CAVERN OF SILVER

JORDAN ALLEN

WALKER AND COMPANY
NEW YORK

To Dorothy

First published in the United States of America in 1982 by the Walker Publishing Company, Inc.

Published simultaneously in Canada by John Wiley & Sons Canada, Limited, Rexdale, Ontario.

ISBN: 0–8027–4014–6

Library of Congress Catalog Card Number: 82–60152

Printed in the United States of America

10   9   8   7   6   5   4   3   2   1

PART 1

CHAPTER 1

PORTER, his big, round body slumped over the littered table, chewed his unlighted cigar from one corner of his thick-lipped mouth to the other and slapped the tabletop with a heavy hand.

"The damn vein's thinned out. Last week I thought it was just a bulge of country rock made it look that way. But it's thinned. They've gone eight feet farther, and it's only six inches wide."

Finley, tall and gaunt with dark, suspicious eyes and drooping black moustache, glanced out the window toward the busy hillside, where lift sheds—like the crests of ant-hills—attracted lines of climbing miners. The muffled clank of stamps shook the ground and air, and the murmur and footsteps of many workingmen formed a constant obbligato.

"Only thing to do is keep diggin' until we see if it's real borasca. Sometimes the veins pinch out, then git big as a room."

Porter looked up at his partner in disgust, his cold little blue eyes contemptuous. "Lucky you know hard-rock minin'," he muttered. "You sure don't know finance."

"What about finance?" Finley countered. "We've been producing."

"And even with a good vein, just about makin' it, payin' back our loan to Bill Sharon. But now, if we're into borasca—"

Finley shrugged, tossed his cigarette to the floor, and pressed out the cigarette with his boot. "So you're telling me

7

we've been living hand to mouth, eh? I suspected as much. But you never made that quite clear, Al. It would have been better if you had. I, for one, don't intend to lose my stake in the Nancy Belle. We've got an agreement."

"Agreements don't mean much if you run out of ore." Porter scraped his chair back on the floor and lifted his big body to a stand.

"Ours does," said Finley quietly. He straightened his tall, bony frame. "I took you at your word—that nobody could lose on this one. You said if I put in my know-how—*and* cash —even if things didn't work out, we'd come out even. I'll hold you to that, Al." He moved a step closer.

Porter glared at him, his large head sunk defiantly between his heavy shoulders. "For God's sake, don't be so simpleminded! A man'll say a lot of things when he's tryin' to sell a deal. You know as well as I do that any proposition is a risk. Well, it looks like on this one we're losin' our shirt and pants!"

Finley's dark eyes hardened, and he reached out and grasped the front of Porter's collar. The fat man's eyes bulged. His face grew red, and he pulled hard at Finley's arm but was unable to loosen his partner's grip.

"Are you crazy?" Porter gasped, his voice half choked.

"No, I'm not crazy," Finley said coolly. "What I *am* saying is that shirt and pants ain't all you're going to lose if this thing turns sour." He released the other man, and Porter fell back into his chair, rubbing his neck and trying to catch his breath.

Finley continued. "You better think up something," he advised. "I've dug the shaft and the drifts and put up the cribbing and mined the ore. You handled the business end. Now it looks like I've handled my end better'n you have yours." He lit another cigarette, leaned across the desk, and blew smoke into his partner's face. "You better think up *something!* And it better work. Don't sell me short—ever!

Porter's desperate gaze clouded as he cogitated. After a

moment he said, "Grant, sit down. We been partners, and up to now things have worked out. You still think that vein might have another bulge?"

"Sure. It might. Look what happened at the Ophir. A second bonanza." His eyes narrowed. "Keep talking."

"If you're sure enough to have us keep diggin', then what we need is money."

Finley was silent, waiting for Porter to continue. The latter's eyes glittered with an idea.

"We may be able to get some," he said thoughtfully. "If we're willin' to take a little chance."

The clank of the stamps and the murmur of the men working on the slopes of Mount Davidson hummed in the background.

"What do you mean—chance?"

"Look, Grant, you told me when you dug Tunnel No. 1—the first one that went south and hit that big chunk of ore—that it went mighty close to Lone Star's Tunnel No. 9."

"Damn close. Stand in ours and you can hear 'em through the rock wall."

"*They're* not in borasca."

"Nope. From what I hear, they're finding forty-dollar ore."

"Right. And what they're findin' is the other end of what we got in our tunnel. Isn't that what you said?"

"I'm sure of it. Ours narrowed, but it's the same vein. But if we go any farther, we'll be into their territory and into their ore. We had a joint survey, it was so close."

Porter leaned back in his chair, recovered his unlit cigar from the floor, and clamped the cigar between his teeth. "Well?" he said and looked directly into his partner's eyes.

"You mean—cross the survey line? Get into Lone Star's ore?"

Porter nodded. "Run another survey. Change the figures."

"I don't like things like that."

Porter shrugged. "It's either that or fold."

Finley stared at him beneath frowning brows. "It's that close?"

"It's that close."

Finley thought a moment, then nodded in a troubled and reluctant manner. "We'll have to be damn careful."

"That's your job. I just finished doin' mine." Porter rubbed his chin. "One thing: We'll need somebody to blame if it gets to court. Somebody to give the wrong order to the drift boss . . ."

CHAPTER 2

VIRGINIA City was a legacy of the gold rush.

When the California placers petered out, and it took money to explore the mother lode in the Sierra, the red-shirted miners who had not struck it rich looked for other treasure troves. Some found their destiny in Australia, some in Mexico and Canada, and some forgot gold for silver when the Comstock exploded into action.

Don Warren stood on C Street and told himself that what he was seeing was hard to believe. Around him teemed a bustling, dusty, raw-timbered town crowded with hurrying humans, honky-tonk piano music pounding from the many saloons, miners in grimy clothing and candle lamps on their caps, some sedate individuals in expensive attire, gleaming boots, and gold watch-chains, burros with X'd *alforjas*, and at that moment a mud-wagon drawn by a six-horse team rattled by.

Above loomed the slopes of Mount Davidson—the mountain of silver—with the burrows and stacks and throngs of men of the Belcher, the Gould & Curry, the Yellow Jacket, and the Mexican—the mines that had struck the first bonanza, with room-size veins of rich silver ore—veins so large that they had to jack up the insides of the mountain, so gargantuan were the sections being hollowed out by eager, delving hands.

Belden Ward had told him in his Montgomery Street office, "Best way to find out what's really going on is to get yourself a job in one of the mines. Not digging—I don't want you to waste your time doing that. In an office somewhere—so you can talk to people."

Warren nodded. He was nearly thirty, dark-haired, smooth-shaven, with intelligent brown eyes, a stubborn jaw, and a wide, generous mouth that smiled easily. He had been born too late for the Rush to California, but he came anyway and took a job with Belden Ward—who hadn't been too late, and who had built his pile into San Francisco real estate and a flour mill and a wharf in the Bay. Warren kept telling himself that there still were opportunities in the West—more than in Zanesville, where he'd been born—but he regretted missing the excitement of the early fifties. And when the great silver strike just across the Sierra burst into flaming action, he was relieved, and he had hinted just enough so that when Ward decided to look into the Comstock, Warren was the logical one to send.

"So you want to know whether it's good, bad, or indifferent, do you . . . and whether things are going up or down?" The younger man's eyes shone with perception.

Ward stroked his graying moustache and grinned understandingly at Warren's enthusiasm. "Yes . . . and you're not going to find out the facts from anybody who thinks you've got money to spend. Listen to the salesmen, sure . . . but don't forget to look behind the scenes. That's why I say to get a job. More chance to find out what's really happening."

"I'll apply for town marshal," Warren chortled. "That'll get me to the scene of action. I better get a gun!" He knew Ward liked him, and he felt privileged enough to joke.

His employer laughed. "That's not the kind of action I'm talking about. All I want you to shoot off is your mouth—asking the right questions. Get a job in a mine office. One of them must need a bookkeeper."

"I still think I'd be a pretty good lawman," Warren boasted. "But I'll do as you say, Mr. Ward." Still he hesitated.

"What is it?" Ward asked.

"You know I'm grateful for this chance, sir," Warren had responded. "But—"

"But what? Don't you want to go? I thought you did."

"I do. But my brother's on his way here. You remember I told you. And I'll be gone when he arrives. He should be here within the week, if the packet from Panama isn't delayed. You promised him a job. Remember? I hope the promise still holds."

"Certainly it holds. I never break my word. Don't worry, my boy. I'll help him get settled, and I'll tell him why you're gone. Can he move into your rooms?"

"Right. That's a load off my mind. Now I'm eager to get started. And—thanks, Mr. Ward. Thanks very much!"

So Don Warren had taken a stage to Sacramento, then another stage to Placerville, then a mud-wagon over Donner Pass—where immigrants had eaten each other in that terrible winter of starvation—and, after some arid, treeless, sunbaked miles, finally into Virginia City and its mountain of silver.

He climbed sweatily to the mine offices.

"No, son, we're laying off office help," said the manager of the Gould & Curry.

"Don't need no more help," said the brusque and officious man at the Belcher.

"Wanta dig? Might use you downstairs," the Yellow Jacket informed him. But Warren shook his head.

"That's not my plate of beans," he said and smiled.

He heard the same story at three other places he went, including the Mexican, and felt a doubt stirring within him that maybe the ore was thinning out. If that were the case, Ward wouldn't be interested. Too bad. He'd hoped to bring back a more encouraging answer. But he needed more facts. Maybe the smaller outfits—

He struck up a conversation with a ponderous Mrs. Emma Nelson, who owned, operated, and lorded it over a restaurant which bore her name, along with the assurance that she served only home-cooked meals.

"Prices is terrible!" the large lady told him as she set before him a massive platter of steak, cabbage, and gravied potatoes. "I'm ashamed to charge a whole dollar for that, but I have to in order to keep goin'. T'won't be long afore the boardin' houses is chargin' five dollars a night. Shameful! But this whole place is goin' wild."

"No sign of the end in sight?" Warren queried.

"Nosirree! People flockin' in here by the hundreds! More money'n you can shake a stick at. And they're findin' more silver all the time." She reached into a canister. "Here. Have a doughnut. On the house. It'll keep up your stren'th."

"Thanks," he said, accepting it. "And they're still finding ore?" He pressed the point, halting a thick piece of steak halfway to his mouth.

"No doubt of it!" She flipped her apron over her arm decisively. "They ain't no end to that ore! Everybody says so."

"I've had trouble finding a job in the bigger outfits."

"Natural!" she scoffed, tossing her head so that her pendulous jowls bounced. "So many people flockin' in here lookin' for jobs, that's why. But it ain't because the ore's pinchin' out. Take my word fer it!" She gazed at him in a kindly fashion. "You know, son," she said thoughtfully, "you might just try some of the smaller outfits—ones just gittin' started. They wun't pay as much, but they wun't have so many askin' 'em fer jobs either."

"Fine," said Warren. "You got the names of some of 'em?"

"Well, there's the Jackdaw, up there beyond the Mexican. And there's the Nancy Belle, up above the Gould & Curry, right next to the Lone Star. You might try there first. The Nancy Belle's closer in, and might strike it richer'n them others."

Warren thanked her, finished his steak, waved his free doughnut at Mrs. Nelson, and, munching it, headed uphill for the Nancy Belle.

*　　*　　*

He was perspiring freely by the time he had tramped up the hill and arrived at the modest unpainted wooden shack which bore the sign, "NANCY BELLE MINE. Porter and Finley, Props." Close by was a black hole in the hillside topped by a lift shed with its steam donkey, its cable drum, and a rickety platform with a handbar for miners to clutch as they dropped into the steamy depths of the mountain. A small ore dump was heaped nearby, and Warren noted that mule carts were used to haul the ore, rather than cars on rails, which were in use in the larger mines.

Not very prepossessing, he thought. He'd rather be with a more prosperous outfit. Shrugging, he entered the office.

There were two desks, one of them a rolltop, and some filing cases. A girl was sitting at the flat desk, working at some papers. There was another inner room in the building, and there was someone inside it, although Warren could not identify the occupant or see him clearly.

At the moment Warren was not interested in the inner office. The girl fully occupied his attention.

She was dark and prim, with a businesslike air. When he entered, she deliberately busied herself with the papers on her desk. Warren felt that she had not been that busy before he opened the door.

She finally looked up. "Yes?" she asked, rather arrogantly, he thought. She had beautifully arched brows, a creamy complexion, and a face that Warren thought was the most perfect oval he had ever seen.

He smiled at her, and his smile was warm and friendly. It had opened many doors for him. He thought he detected a softening of her mood. "I'm looking for a job," he confessed. "Are Mr. Porter or Mr. Finley here?"

She unbent a trifle. He found himself admiring her mouth as she spoke. "I doubt very much if there's a job to be had. But Mr. Porter's here. I'll tell him about you." She rose and moved briskly, with a rustling of skirts, to the inner office. She carefully closed the door behind her, and from within he heard the murmur of voices. In a moment she was out, looking rather surprised, he thought.

"Mr. Porter will see you," she told him. She shrugged as she seated herself again at the desk, still primly erect. "It's certainly a change from what he told me the other day."

"I'm sure he couldn't have told you anything unpleasant," Warren said.

She cast a puzzled glance at him.

He smiled again and explained. "No one could possibly be unpleasant to anyone as pretty as you." He was somewhat surprised at his own boldness.

She reddened and turned away, embarrassed. "Mr. Porter is waiting."

Warren went through the swinging gate, rounded her desk, and entered the inner office. Crouched over a littered desk, he saw a corpulent man with mussed hair, wrinkled clothes, a red face, and an unlighted cigar in the corner of his mouth. The man regarded his visitor with little blue eyes that were cold and appraising.

"Miss Finley tells me you're lookin' for work."

Miss Finley. Obviously she was related to one of the owners, but it was "Miss," so she was not his wife.

"I am, sir," Warren said. He was not offered a chair, so he stood before the desk, looking down at the big, unkempt man.

"You're not after a diggin' job?"

"No, I'm after an office job. I've had experience. I've been a bookkeeper. I've supervised an office."

Porter was silent for a long moment, gazing sharply and fixedly at his visitor. He seemed to be trying to determine exactly what kind of person he was. He chewed the cigar thoughtfully from one corner of his mouth to the other.

"Supervised an office, eh?"

"Yes, sir. Belden Ward's, in San Francisco."

Porter nodded. "I've heard of Ward. Got his finger in a lot of pies."

Warren agreed noncommittally. "He's successful." Nor did he disclose the fact that he still was in Ward's employ.

"Well—" Porter rubbed his fat chin and spoke slowly, as if he were making up his mind. "Why are you leaving Ward?"

"I'm not being fired, if that's what you mean. This seems to be where there's a lot of action. Thought I'd try my luck in the Comstock. A fellow never gets anywhere staying in one place."

The statement seemed to satisfy Porter. He nodded. "I like young fellers with git-up-and-go. Well, son, we might just have somethin' for you. My pard is the minin' expert, and I'm the businessman. But we need somebody to keep track of the men and the wages and how much we're producin'. To be sort of a straw boss. Interested?"

Warren was relieved. This was exactly what he wanted. It would give him the base from which to find out what really was going on in Virginia City—and the pretty girl in the office was no deterrent. Still, he felt that he must not appear too anxious.

"Sounds good . . . but it depends on the pay. How much?"

Porter's eyes narrowed. "If you're the kind of young feller I think you are, I'll offer you somethin'. And if you're smart, you'll take it."

"What is it?"

"Low pay, and a share in the mine."

"What's low, and what's the share amount to?"

"Eighty a month . . . and 1 percent of the net."

Warren pretended to hesitate. "The mine's doing well?"

"Would I be hirin' you if we weren't?"

"Make it 2 percent and I'll take it."

"Good!" said Porter without hesitation. He heaved himself erect, reached across the desk with his thick hand, and shook Warren's. "It's a deal. When can you start?"

"Soon as I get me some digs to sleep in. I can start today."

"There's a roomin' house down the street, right next to

Emma Nelson's cafe. Come on back as soon as you're settled, and we'll start you out."

"Fine! I'll do a good job for you." Warren made his exit, halted at Miss Finley's desk, and told her, "I'm hired. Guess we'll be working together." And he smiled.

"Well . . ." She seemed more surprised than before.

Whistling as he left the office, her large, dark eyes remained in his memory.

Finley—tall and dark, with wet clay on his boots—entered the office a few moments later. He was scowling. The girl looked up. "Uncle Grant," she said, "Mr. Porter just hired somebody new. I thought things weren't going so well and we were firing people, not hiring them—"

Finley grunted. "I just been down to drift No. 3. It's borasca, all right. Vein's pinching out fast. A new man, eh? I'll talk to Al and see what's up. Maybe we could use somebody at that . . . in the office, not in the mine. We don't plan to go out of business just yet."

He went into the inner office, surprisingly, the girl thought, closing the door carefully after him. She heard voices and Porter's heavy laugh, and she thought she heard him say, "Grant, we got our pigeon."

She returned thoughtfully to her desk. Her uncle was not in the habit of confiding in her, but both he and Porter had been complaining lately about the thinning ore. If she had heard him correctly, what did Porter's statement mean? A pigeon? Whose pigeon? And why? And the young man—although he seemed overly sure of himself—had had a very nice smile.

She returned to her work, frowning. She was puzzled and felt a vague sense of unease. . . .

Don Warren went back to the rooming house next to Emma Nelson's cafe and became a lodger for thirty dollars a month —in advance. Then he went next door and sought the ponderous Mrs. Nelson.

"I got the job," he told her. "Thanks for the advice."

"Where?"

"At the Nancy Belle. They hired me straight off."

"Good!" She beamed, pleasure crinkling her eyes and producing two large and surprising dimples in her heavy cheeks. "Here! Have a doughnut to celebrate!"

He laughed and accepted the gift. "I'll be eating here regularly," he told her. "You're responsible for my career."

She erased her smile and became serious. "Met Finley's niece yet?" she inquired.

He grinned broadly. "I sure have! And she's mighty good to look at. What do you know about her?"

"Well . . ." Mrs. Nelson frowned speculatively, "not much. She come out here because she's a orphan, and she wrote Finley and ast if he had a job for her. Ohio wasn't offerin' much in the way of jobs fer women."

"She's from Ohio?"

"Columbus."

"I'm from Zanesville."

"Well! Yer damn near neighbors! Anyways, from what I hear, she ain't gettin' along so good with her relative. Both he and his pardner, Al Porter, are tough *hombres*. A lot of drinkin', a lot of carousin'."

Warren raised his brows. "And the girl?"

"She ain't that kind. She don't approve. But she's workin' for 'em, and he's her uncle."

He finished the doughnut and smiled at her again. She melted, and again the surprising dimples appeared. "Thanks," he told her. "I'm grateful, and you'll see me often."

"Can't be often enough!" It was almost a simper.

Once out the door, he made his way up the hill toward the Nancy Belle. The problems of the Nancy Belle, he reflected, might be more interesting than the status of the silver lode in Mount Davidson. But he had been hired to be interested in the latter—and he was not disposed to shirk his responsibilities.

He whistled as he climbed the hill. . . .

* * *

When he arrived at the Nancy Belle's headquarters building, neither Porter nor Finley was there. He was somewhat surprised at this, recalling that he had told Porter that he would be back immediately . . . but he needn't have been. The partners had left the office for C Street, where the bars were, and were deep in conversation in the Oriental over glasses of Bourbon which had come around the Horn from Kentucky via the Mississippi, New Orleans, and San Francisco.

"He's just what we been lookin' for!" Porter said, taking the unlighted cigar from his mouth and gesturing with it. "Greener than grass! He don't know which end the jackass kicks from. Been workin' in an office in San Francisco, and said he supervised an office staff. That's jest what we want! We'll tell him to make sure we clean out all the ore from every drift, and we'll feed him stuff from the eight-hundred level. It'll be some time before we're caught, and when we are—*if* we are—all the records'll be in his desk. He's the one who'll have given the orders. They can't touch us . . . and by that time it'll be too late."

Finley was doubtful. He lit a cigar and sipped his whiskey. "How can you be so sure? You just met this feller."

"He's green, I tell you! A smooth-faced kid! We'll walk all over him!"

Finley grunted. "I hope you're right. We're having enough trouble with my niece. I wish to hell she'd never shown up. But she's here . . . so we'll have to make arrangements."

Porter leered. "Purty gal. A real nice filly."

Finley reddened with anger. "You keep your dirty paws off her, you hear? One misstep and I'll slice your liver!"

Porter again chewed his cigar from one side of his mouth to the other and raised his hands in mock surrender. "Down, boy! Nobody's steppin' out of line! Back off, I say! If I want a woman, I'm not goin' after one of your relations!"

Finley glared at him. "See that you don't! I mean it!"

The big man cast a cryptic glance at his partner, then tried to return the conversation to the previous topic. "I think we ought to give the kid a job with a high-soundin' title so's there won't be no question about his authority over whatever we want him to do."

Finley tugged at his chin. "Whatever you say," he grunted.

"We'll call him supervisor. That'll cover whatever happens."

Again Finley grunted.

That evening Don Warren sat before the fire and composed a letter to Belden Ward.

Dear Mr. Ward:

This is to apprise you that I have done what you instructed me to do, and, of a consequence, I feel that I am in a most favorable position to give you reliable information as to what is going on in the Comstock.

For a while I despaired of getting a job, but I am happy to report that I have been employed at the Nancy Belle mine, Porter and Finley, Props. It is a smaller operation—not the scale of the Gould & Curry or the Ophir—and because of it, it may be more sensitive to the true activity in the lode.

There is considerable talk that the lode may be pinching out. They call it "going into borasca," or thin ore. Businesspeople want to squelch such talk, and, in view of the fact that I got the job, it is possible the situation is not pessimistic. However, I still have the question as to why the big mines are not hiring, and the little one did.

I promise to keep you informed. My most cordial wishes to Mrs. Ward.

Your ob't. servant,

Donald Warren

When Ward received it, he thoughtfully tapped the letter on his knee. A medium-sized, squarely built man with iron-gray hair and an iron-gray moustache, his blue eyes were frank, honest, and inquiring. His clothing was expensive, his boots of polished cordovan leather, and his watch chain was heavy and of solid gold.

He called his male secretary into his office. "Gaines," he said, "haven't we heard of somebody named Porter? Or Finley?"

The secretary—a studious, stooped young man with an intense expression—frowned in concentration. "The names do sound familiar, sir. But for the life of me, I can't place them at this moment."

"Keep thinking," Ward advised. "So will I."

"Indeed I will, sir." And the secretary ducked his head and left the room.

Alone, Belden Ward rose and walked to a window overlooking Montgomery Street. He saw wagons and carriages, and scurrying men and women. Hurrying seemed to be a characteristic of San Franciscans! And buildings were being hammered up—the tent-topped unpainted shacks of the fifties being rapidly replaced by more permanent structures. San Francisco was becoming a real city!

Porter . . . He said the name over to himself. It sounded familiar, he thought. And Finley. Not as familiar . . . but some vague memory jogged his thoughts. Belden Ward was irritated. He prided himself on his memory, and in this case it was failing him. But he would keep thinking, and sooner or later he would remember. In time he hoped to get in touch with Don Warren—in case the memory portended any trouble.

Ward returned to his desk and picked up the other letter that had arrived that morning. As he reread it, he smiled.

Dear Sir:

You may be interested to know that the conversations that have occurred between us gave rise to a board discussion last Tuesday. As a result, we in this office may be interested in further talk relating to a possible sale of our properties to you.

Will you be so kind as to drop in or write at your convenience?

Yours very sincerely,

James Y. Cobden
Managing Director
Lone Star Mine
Virginia City, Nevada

Putting down the letter, Belden Ward called his secretary and bade him inform Mr. Cobden that the conversations could continue—indeed, should—at the earliest possible date.

CHAPTER 3

THAT evening Don Warren strolled down C Street in Virginia City to watch what was happening.

A lot *was* happening. Miners, dirty and clay-covered, weary from long hours in the overheated stopes and drifts of the mines, came to town to relax and raise hell.

Others eagerly awaited them. Dark-clad, smooth-faced gamblers, riffling decks of cards in supple fingers, tempted them to poker or faro tables. Bartenders—heavy moustaches seemed to be a mark of their trade—stood ready to welcome them with racks of gleaming bottles and glittering glasses. Girls—some pretty, some not, but all willing—flounced ruffled skirts and bent over seated males, wearing décolletage that drooped lower than anything east of the Mississippi. Piano players—many of whom had sacrificed musical careers in the East because of undue affection for the bottle—pounded untuned pianos between drinks and kept a cacophony of tinny sound rattling between the bars of the town, merging in a wild, indistinguishable crescendo that hovered over Virginia City like a thunderous cloud.

And the people! Don Warren had seen the mixture of races in San Francisco. But Virginia City offered a mélange of races and types that not only fascinated him but also disturbed him. He had never known the human race could encompass such extremes.

There were white men—and women, of a type. There were Mexicans—proud and erect of carriage, looking with a degree

24

of disdain on what was happening but aware of the necessity to get into it if they were to survive and prosper. There were Chinese in slippers and smocks, robes and skullcaps, who moved with businesslike mien, because they were engaged in business. Their laundries, stores, and restaurants had names like Hop Sing, Liu, and Chiang over their doors. And—more than anyone else—there were large numbers of newly arrived Irishmen.

Don Warren looked at the scene and studied it, a scene composed of so many facets of human existence. Then he sighed and grinned to himself as he halted before a pleasure emporium labeled the Oriental. It had swinging doors, and he pushed both of them open to find himself in a raw-timbered room filled with a hundred or more people, some standing by a long bar, lifting glasses repetitively to their lips; some crouched around circular tables with green baize covers, frowning over hands of cards; some devoting attention to colorfully clad dancing girls who sat on the arms of their chairs, twining their slim fingers in greasy locks of hair, encouraging them to spend and spend and spend . . .

Warren walked up to the bar, and when the rotund bartender condescended to pay him heed, he ordered a whiskey with water.

The man behind the counter apparently was not pleased. "Any special kind?" he asked contemptuously.

"A good kind," Warren shrugged. "None of the sewage you serve your regular customers."

The answer commanded new respect. Reaching high on a shelf for a bottle, the bartender filled a small glass and set it before the man he had never seen before.

"You forgot the water," Warren reminded him.

"Sorry," the barkeep responded. Hustling to the end of the bar, he obliged by drawing a glass from a spigot on a barrel.

Warren paid the two dollars for it and looked around. Next to him stood a shaggy-haired man with a grizzled beard, weather-stained slouch hat, red-veined nose, and a thick, muscular body. The man was grinning at him—but he detected that the grin was not friendly. Raising his glass before him, the shaggy one muttered, "Hafta water yer drinks, hey? Weak stummick, or weak character?"

Warren was aware that the man was in his cups and spoiling for an argument. So he turned away. "I like it that way," he said over his shoulder. "Any objections?"

"Yeah," the man bellowed, with obvious intent to be irritating. "We don't want Sadies in Virginia. This is a *man's* town."

For a moment Warren debated with himself as to how to answer the fellow. From the corner of his eye he could see that several onlookers were watching and listening with interest, apparently anticipating a fight.

Choosing to ignore him, he turned his back, directing his attention to the other end of the bar, where two miners already were in the middle of a noisy argument. But the shaggy man was not disposed to let him off so easily. A hard finger prodded Warren in the back, and a drunken voice insisted, "Look, Sadie, if'n you cain't take yer liquor straight, better git out of town! I'll he'p you—"

There was nothing to do but turn around to face his annoyer.

"Look," Warren said, attempting to disarm his antagonist, "you drink the way you want. I'll drink the way I want. All right?"

The man grew ugly. His face was red and his little eyes shone with drunken belligerence. "*Not* all right!" He swung around. "Fellers, we got a Sadie here!" he cried, raising his voice. "A real soft-fingered lollapalooza of a Sadie! Let's run him out of town!"

A crowd began to gather. Warren sensed that no one was responding to the invitation to run him out of town—but they *were* expecting him to answer the challenge. A soft answer would no longer be effective.

Carefully he sized up his opponent. A man, probably in his forties, with early graying hair, who was obviously physically hard as nails. Muscles bulged on his arms, and his weathered complexion betokened days and nights in the open. As for Warren, he had tried boxing in Zanesville in an athletic club which had been opened by a man who styled himself an "athletic coach and prize fighter from New York, New Jersey, and the European nations." Dutifully, along with most other young men in Zanesville, Warren had taken lessons, listened to advice, lost a friend by pounding him too enthusiastically in a match hovered over by the athletic coach with European experience—then dropped the activity when the coach, who had not paid a single bill since he arrived, suddenly left town.

Warren doubted that this slight training made him a match for the muscular drunk, spoiling for a fight, who faced him. But there seemed to be no way of avoiding a crucial test of his Zanesville curriculum.

Carefully, he set his glass on the counter; then, without warning, he drove his right fist as hard as he could into the shaggy one's solar plexus.

Uttering a muffled "Whoof!" the man bent over, dropping his glass on the floor, where it shattered and spattered whiskey over Warren's boots. As the crowd gaped, the downed man pressed both hands to his stomach, groaned, and found he could not straighten up.

Warren considered the situation briefly, then acted. Sure in his decision, he lifted his right knee, hard, to the man's jaw. The big one went over backward, crashing into a barroom chair—and lay there, knees up, still clutching his stomach and trying to catch his breath.

Again Warren considered. The crowd encircling the two was silent, watching. If he waited until his opponent recovered, he would be sure to be beaten or shot. A glance at the crowd told him so—that it was a battery of cruel, bloodthirsty eyes, hungry for violence. The reputation a man made in this town was important, he decided. He either would be respected or given trouble. His own stature was being tested. He would leave the Oriental in one of two ways: either beaten and derided, unable to fulfill his boss's assignment; or with a measure of respect, no longer in danger of being the butt of oafish frontier humor.

He suddenly leaped forward, jumping with both feet, encased as they were in heavy boots, onto the man's stomach. The man roared with pain, rolling over and over, groaning. Warren then picked up the chair which his enemy had overturned, lifted it high, and smashed it on the man's head. He hoped he had not cracked his skull.

The man's thick hat offered some protection, but not enough to keep him from being knocked senseless, and the hard-muscled, grizzled drunk collapsed in a motionless heap on the floor.

Trying not to let his thumping pulse show, Warren sauntered to the bar and, with an affected air of nonchalance, jerked a thumb at his fallen foe. "Throw some water on that slug," he told the bartender. "And when he comes to, tell him—from now on—to keep out of my way!"

Tossing off his drink, he settled his hat more firmly on his head and made his way through the awestruck crowd, which quickly opened a path for him. But when he reached the street, he realized he had forgotten to pay for his drink. So he pushed back again through the swinging doors, and this time tossed two coins at the bartender, saying, "Here, catch!" before he made his final exit.

Back in his room in the boardinghouse next to Emma Nelson's cafe, he sat down shakily in the only wooden chair, tossed his hat on the wrinkled bed, and mopped his perspiring brow with a blue bandanna.

He had, he realized, been inordinately lucky. His opponent had been bigger and stronger than he, and in a fair fight he most assuredly would have been beaten to a bloody pulp. He had not fought fair. But somehow he did not feel that that disqualified him from the town's respect. Virginia City was a tough place.

Gradually, his trembling nerves quieted and he began to breathe more evenly. And as he did so, he began to feel a certain satisfaction. The Comstock had not waited long to test him out . . . and he had not come out badly. He was grateful that he had had sense enough to return to pay his tab. That one act defined him as an honest man. He was a man who might jump on a man's stomach and knee him in the jaw, but he paid for his drinks.

The more he thought about the fray, the better he felt about it. He hoped he had not hurt the drunk seriously, but comforted himself with the thought that the man would have mauled him if it had been the other way around.

To break him into his new job at the Nancy Belle, Grant Finley took Don Warren through the mine.

Warren had heard about the Comstock mines—the heat in the lower depths; the boiling water that poured from underground springs, scalding screaming men to death in the blackness of the lower levels; the elevators that sometimes broke loose from their cables, dropping like stones and crashing their human load into a bloody pulp at the shaft bottom. And the Nancy Belle fulfilled all his expectations.

He and Finley climbed up the steep slope, the sun hot on their backs, to the little shed which covered the steam donkey engine and the shaft entrance. The elevator—held by a single wire cable which ran to a drum revolving above their heads at the apex of an inverted V-frame—was a simple wooden platform about four feet square, with two pipes bolted vertically at the sides. Another pipe, connecting their tops, served as a handhold. There was no barrier around the elevator's sides, and if one stepped backward, it was into the black depths of the thousand-foot shaft.

"Come on," Finley invited, stepping onto the elevator platform. "Let's take a quick look below."

Warren joined him, but with some misgivings. For one thing, the lift shook as he mounted it. And it seemed too flimsy. He gripped the pipe crossbar—with both hands.

Finley noted his unsureness and grinned, trying to hide it beneath his black moustache. He jerked a thumb at the donkeyman and, as he did so, suddenly the bottom dropped out of Don Warren's world. The elevator platform plummeted downward into utter blackness. It felt as if the engineman had simply turned off the power and let the elevator drop freely. It was a sickening sensation, and Warren's stomach rose into his throat and his head whirled. Then, suddenly—so suddenly that his knees bent and he almost lost his footing—the elevator braked to a halt, trembling and shaking, bouncing on its cable, at the entrance to a black hole in the side of the shaft.

He was wearing a candle cap, and so was Finley—and when Finley stepped off the elevator, Warren followed him by the light from his cap. "Come on," Finley encouraged. "We're at Drift One. Would you believe? It's the eight-hundred-foot level."

Still trying to force his stomach down, Warren followed, gingerly.

The first thing he noticed was the heat. It was terribly hot—a steamy kind of heat that almost choked off his breath. In a moment he was dripping with perspiration—not the kind of sun sweat that oozed from his pores and dried immediately when he was in the desert, but a drenching, clinging perspiration that damped and slowed his every move.

Ahead in the distance were flickering lights and, as they walked toward them, candles in wall sconces illumined rough walls which, in some places, dripped with steamy water. For what seemed a quarter of a mile to him, they proceeded down the dark and eerie drift until at the tunnel's end they came upon a dozen men.

The miners were shirtless, some clad only in breechclouts and heavy shoes. All were wet and gleaming with perspiration, and they stared and nodded at Finley, but did not cease—or even pause in—their work. Warren's eye went to the drift boss, a thin, pug-nosed Irishman in ragged dungarees with a candle cap bigger than the rest, and while Warren watched him, the man shouted an order. It was clearly welcome, for before it was out of his mouth, the men had thrown down their tools and scrambled for the elevator.

Smiling, the drift boss approached them and raised a hand to Finley. "Glad to see ye, sir," he greeted. "Does us all good to see the big boss come down here once in a while."

In acknowledgment, Finley grunted. "We work 'em only two hours at a time," he explained to Warren. "It's too damn hot for 'em to stay longer." Thinking of the amenities, he gestured toward Warren. "This is the new supervisor, Pat," he said. "Mr. Warren, meet Pat Flaherty."

The two shook sweaty hands, and Warren felt an immediate liking for the tall, grinning miner with the sweat-streaked countenance. But in the distance, as the elevator growled upward, Warren felt a sudden clutch of fear. Down here in the bowels of the earth, what if the elevator engine failed? They'd be down here cooking for hours. . . .

As Finley and Flaherty talked, Warren was relieved to hear the elevator descend again. He heard the tramp of feet through the drift. The next shift of a dozen men arrived, laughing and joking. They stripped off their shirts, some their pants as well, and the whole process began again.

"How close are you to the Lone Star?" Finley asked Pat.

Motioning them to come closer to the end of the drift, Flaherty cocked a head toward the rocky wall. "Hark!" he said. The two did—and even over the sounds of the picks of the miners around them, they could hear the muffled thumps and bumps of men working the other side of the rocky barrier.

"It's a crime," Flaherty said. "This vein's thin, but it's a'widenin' out. Lone Star's workin' the other side, and I bet it's as big as a room. Fifty feet more and we'd be in their territory. Bet we'd be in bonanza ore."

Finley rubbed his chin thoughtfully. "I've been thinking of

having this hole resurveyed," he said. He peered closely again at the vein. It was six inches wide, in spots more than a foot, the wider spots toward the end of the drift. "We may have some of that bonanza on our side of the line," he speculated. He turned to Warren. "You understand? This vein's widening, and we've got to get every inch of it that's ours. I'm going over those survey figures again. . . ."

Flaherty shook his large head. "T'won't do no good," he assured. "I've gone over your figures, Grant, and they're right. We can't push much farther, or we'll be in the Lone Star."

Finley eyed him stubbornly. "I'm going over the figures again, I tell you. We're not going to miss a trick!"

"T'won't do no good," Flaherty repeated patronizingly. "Waste o' time."

The conversation ended. Flaherty led them back toward the elevator, pointing out a wet spot in the wall where water had seeped and dripped into a puddle on the floor.

"The damn hot water," he said. "If'n you stick yer pick into the wrong place, it'll spout out at ye like Niagara—hot enough to b'il eggs! If ye git caught, ye don't drown, ye git scalded to death! Sutro ought to dig his drain tunnel now. . . ."

Finley shrugged. "Longer we can get along without Sutro, the better. He wants two dollars off the top for every ton of ore."

At the shaft, where Finley pulled a signal cord to have the elevator descend for them, Flaherty asked him flatly, "Are ye goin' to dig deeper?"

The mine owner grinned mirthlessly. "What's the matter?" he asked. "You sound as if you're not enthusiastic."

"I ain't," said the Irishman unequivocally. "And I'll tell ye why. The deeper ye go, the more miserable it gits. So damn hot ye can't touch the tools! And for what? Are there any signs of ore below?"

"Some," said Finley. "But your job's to drive this drift all the way to the heavy ore next to the Lone Star." He whirled around to Warren. "And now it's your job too. Our first priority's to get all that's coming to us. After that, we can think of digging deeper."

Flaherty sighed openly. "Maybe we'll find the bonanza we're lookin' for," he said, "right here at this level. But I doubt it. That'll be Lone Star's luck."

As the elevator platform rattled down to a shaking halt before them, Warren stepped aboard eagerly and Finley followed, jerking his head at the Irishman. "We *better* find it at this level," he said as he tugged at the signal cord.

The elevator responded, jumping upward, almost knocking Warren from the platform. It rose with sickening speed, sending his stomach as far toward his boots as it had lifted it toward his throat on the descent. Swiftly the air cooled, and at the surface the bright sunlight suddenly blinded him, but the hot sunlight and the dry air were quickly refreshing.

As they walked, slipping and sliding in the dust, down the steep hill toward the office, Finley called to Warren over his shoulder, "We've got to get that drift as close to the Lone Star's as we can. That's your first job."

"But what about the survey?" Warren panted.

"Count on me to get the figures," Finley told him. At that moment the two entered the building.

His job at the Nancy Belle, Warren found, was no picnic.

Porter and Finley, Props., worried little about record-keeping, accounts, or an orderly office. Miss Finley—whose first name, he found out, was Sarah—kept the only neat desk in the place, and she was as baffled and as troubled as he by the disorderly procedures.

Al Porter's instructions to him had been simple. "You run the office, Warren," he had told him. "Our books ain't been kept up right, and we've just split the take between us every week, in cash. See if you can straighten 'em out."

Warren went at the job and found it most difficult. The entries were simple enough—so many tons of ore each week at $25.00, $32.00, or $40.00 a ton assay, the total then added up—and when they got the cash from Bill Sharon's mill, after they'd paid the milling charge, they had a simple entry:

P—$520.00
F—$520.00

with a date.

After sweating over the tangled accounts for three days, Warren went to Porter and said, "I've got a report to make, and I think you'll be interested in it."

Porter chewed his cigar from one side of his mouth to the other and shook his head. "I ain't interested in any reports," he said. "Just keep your nose in them books and straighten 'em out in case any bankers or tax collectors start askin' questions."

"I still think you'll be interested," Warren persisted, standing in front of Porter's littered desk.

"I said I wasn't, kid." Porter's cold little blue eyes were hostile. "If you want this job, do what I tell ya."

Warren stood his ground. "You've been swindled by Sharon's mill," he said quietly. "He owes you money. Eight thousand, in fact."

There was a long silence. Porter took the cigar from his mouth and regarded Warren fixedly. "We ain't been swindled by Bill Sharon," he said slowly. "He's an honest man."

"I still say he owes you eight thousand dollars, and I can prove it by these accounts. He's overcharged you, ton by ton."

Porter lifted his gross bulk from behind the desk, replaced the cigar in the corner of his mouth, and rounded the desk. His mood suddenly changed. He laid a fat hand on Warren's shoulder. "Look, son," he said pleasantly, "our accounts ain't all they should be. You know that. But I'll lay my right hand to your left foot that Bill Sharon ain't swindled us out of a nickel. Why would he need to? He represents the Bank of California, and he's the richest man in the Comstock. Come on, let's have a look at them books."

Together they bent over the accounts. Warren was unpleasantly conscious of the huge, sweaty man next to him.

Porter breathed heavily, wheezing at times, and the odorous, chewed cigar wafted effluvia toward him that was nauseating.

"Here's what I'm talking about," Warren said, pointing at a column of expenses. "According to the rate page, Sharon's supposed to be charging you so much a ton for milling, but when I figured it out, he's really overcharging you nine dollars a ton."

Porter laughed heavily and straightened up. "Is that all?" he said. "The answer to that is easy. Those rates change week by week. That rate list ain't up to date."

"Yes, it is, Mr. Porter," Warren said, and he began to eye the big man with interest. "I checked at the mill. And for these weeks in question, it was strictly according to the rate schedule, which hasn't been changed in four months."

Porter's mood altered again. He moved heavily back behind his desk and stood there glaring at Warren. "Look, kid," he said, "I hired you to run the office and keep books. If I've had to make a payoff once in a while to keep certain people friendly, that's none o' your business. The last thing the Nancy Belle needs is a row with Bill Sharon and the bank."

So there had been a payoff! Warren suddenly knew why Porter wanted no row with Sharon.

"If there's been a payoff, how do I adjust the accounts?" Warren asked stiffly.

"Leave 'em the way they are," Porter instructed. "Don't change a line. Leave 'em the way they are. And what we've just talked about ain't safe to go blatherin' about. Keep it under your hat, kid. I mean it. Nobody accuses Bill Sharon —or me—of anything like that and stays healthy."

He remained standing until Warren left the office. And even as he departed, Warren felt Porter's hostile little blue eyes boring into his back.

Warren worked for the rest of the day with much on his mind. So there had been payoffs! He had heard much of Sharon, the "king of the Comstock," the agent of the powerful Bank of California, which had bankrolled most of the mines and mills on Sun Mountain. Sharon, it was reported, was the personal representative of William Ralston, cashier of the Bank of California and master of its destinies. Together, Sharon and Ralston had bet on the Comstock, and the bet had paid off. They had made millions—for themselves, for the stockholders in the mines. But they had gambled with their depositors' money. At least that was the way Belden Ward looked at it.

Maybe Warren had discovered another reason why Sharon was wealthy. Maybe Sharon took payoffs.

But why should he? Why should a multimillionaire who was making legitimate dollars so fast he could not count them take the risk of a bribery scandal? Warren shook his head and leaned back in his chair at the rolltop desk. In doing so he had a fine view of Sarah Finley's straight, prim back, her long, dark hair piled attractively and neatly on her head, the crisp, white, high-necked, long-sleeved blouse she wore, and her unremitting attention to her work.

That attention never had wavered since Don Warren had assumed his place at the rolltop. She was courteous to him, almost friendly—but forbiddingly proper. And during working hours her conversation was strictly limited.

Today, he felt, there was the need to talk. If Porter were making payoffs to Sharon, Finley should know it. But did he?

And *was* Porter making payoffs to Sharon? Of all the people in the Comstock, Sharon needed payoffs less than anyone.

Warren rose from his desk and cleared his throat. "Miss Finley," he said. She stopped work but did not turn around. "Miss Finley," he repeated, "I would like to have a little talk with you."

"These are working hours, Mr. Warren," she reminded him, still not turning around.

"I assure you this is not social," he said. "And I want to speak to you while Mr. Porter is out of the office."

She swung around on her chair and faced him, back erect, her expression severe.

He sat down on a corner of his desk and regarded her with appreciation. Dark hair, creamy skin, dark eyes, a mouth that could smile but was unaccustomed to it, a crisp, freshly laundered blouse and pressed skirt—Miss Finley clearly was not going to permit the Comstock to alter her style.

"Well?" she said, almost challenging.

"Why are you so unfriendly?" he asked.

She sighed. "Mr. Warren," she said, "you assured me this was not to be a social chat."

Her stiffness, he concluded, probably was because she had been accosted by a number of impossible people since she had come West, and she was not disposed to encourage a soul.

"I want to talk to you about something very serious."

"Well, what is it?" she asked.

He told her about his telling Porter that he suspected Sharon of padding the milling charges. She listened. He told her about Porter's attempt to discount the whole thing, then about Porter's turning around and admitting that he was making payoffs.

"Does your uncle know Porter's making payoffs?" he asked in conclusion.

She was shocked, and she showed it. "He's—he's never mentioned it to me," she said. "But—Uncle Grant seldom talks to me about business. Maybe we ought to tell him."

"We certainly should," Warren agreed with enthusiasm. "But if we do, I want to tell him something else."

"What else is there?"

"I want to tell him something that could cost me my job if I'm wrong. And I want you to tell me whether I ought to tell him or not—based on what you know about how your uncle and Porter get along."

Warren gazed into her attractive face and thought hard for a moment. Could he trust her? If he could not—if she were aware of what was going on, despite her look of surprise—if Porter and Finley actually were partners in all that went on—then his usefulness to Belden Ward would be ended. In addition, he might get shot. There were killings daily in Virginia City, and he already had classified Porter as one with a limited number of scruples.

She shifted impatiently in her chair, and a pretty frown creased her otherwise smooth brow. "Well, are you going to say something or not?" she asked as she waited for him to speak.

He made his decision, hoping it was not influenced too much by her beauty. This could turn out wrong, but he did not think it would. He took a deep breath.

"I don't think Porter is making payoffs to Sharon," he began. "But before I tell you what I think, would you tell me—and tell me honestly—if your uncle and Porter get along well together. Think hard. Are they friendly, or do they mistrust each other? And have you sensed any suspicion between them? Are they friends, or are they just working together?"

She started to speak, then hesitated as she saw the intensity of his expression. He could see that she was thinking hard. Was she doing as he asked, or was she figuring how to deceive him?

Finally she spoke. "I honestly don't know," she said. "I don't think there's any love lost between them. They go out and have a drink together occasionally, but they're pretty stiff with each other. They've had a couple of arguments since I've been here. But they've been in the inner office with the door closed, and I couldn't hear what they were saying, just loud voices. But even married people argue sometimes, so I don't know what that means in terms of their relationship. But—but why should I be telling you all this? What's on your mind?"

Don Warren decided that she was being straightforward with him and, along with it, he realized that it presented a problem to her too. After all, he was a rank newcomer—and she was the niece of one of the partners.

"I'll tell you what's on your mind," he said flatly. "I don't think Porter's paying Sharon off. I think he's paying himself off. If your uncle doesn't know it, he should. If he does—and we tell him—there goes my job!"

The girl digested this information silently, then rose and came closer. "I don't know whether Uncle Grant knows it or not," she admitted. "But if it's really happening . . . can you prove it?"

He spent the next twenty minutes showing her the books that he had shown Porter. "Porter admitted there'd been payoffs," he said. "But he implied they were to Bill Sharon—and he warned me that Sharon would be a bad man to tangle with if the word ever got out. Let me ask it this way: If Porter *has* been taking a cut off the top for himself on the milling charges, is your uncle a party to it?"

"I have no reason to think he's dishonest," she said slowly. "But then, I really don't know him very well."

If there had been any doubt in Warren's mind as to her willingness to confide in him, her uncertain manner convinced him of her frankness. She was deeply disturbed at the news he had brought her, and he perceived a single question running through her mind: Is there *no one* I can trust on this raw frontier, not even my uncle?

"Well," he said at last, "I'll leave it up to you to decide whether to tell him. You know him better than I. But I thought I should tell you what I suspect."

The stiffness was gone. Her dark eyes were confiding. He could see that she now regarded him as a friend.

"I'll . . . I'll think about it. Oh, I must think about it," she said. "And thank you for telling me."

They both turned back to their work, but Warren was conscious of the disappearance of the cloud of formality that had hovered over the office since his arrival. The girl said nothing, but there was no shuffling of papers, no scratching of a pen. She was not working. She was sitting there thinking.

After a time he swung around again in his chair and faced her. "You know, if you don't mind steak," he blurted out, "I'll take you to Emma Nelson's for lunch. She's good for the troubled spirit."

For the first time, Sarah Finley smiled at him. "I know she is," she said. "I've talked with her. All right, Mr. Warren, I'll be glad to accept your invitation to lunch—and maybe afterward, I can decide what to do."

Side by side, they walked down the slope of Sun Mountain toward C Street and the bustling, boisterous center of Virginia City.

"What are you doing here?" he asked as they strolled along. "You look like a city girl to me."

"Well, Columbus hardly is a big city, but it's civilized. That's more than you can say for this—" She waved a hand at the red-shirted, Levi-clad, booted miners; the Chinese in their robes and slippers and pigtails; the Mexicans under their broad-brimmed sombreros and silver-buttoned vests and *pantalónes*. The Oriental saloon loomed before them, and shouts and sounds of breaking glass and furniture emerged from the doorway. They halted just as a man smashed through the batwings and rolled in a back somersault in the street. He rose, his expression fierce, brushed himself off, and plunged again into the saloon, where loud voices again shook the windowpanes.

Don Warren laughed and hurried the girl past the doorway.

"I'm here," she answered as their pace slowed again, "because Uncle Grant's my only living relative. I'm an orphan—and now that I'm grown, I don't want to be a burden on the family that took care of me. But I hated to leave them!" she said, a tear glistening in her eye. "And they didn't want me to. They were wonderful!"

At the cafe, Emma Nelson produced a hearty lunch, as expected—far more than the girl could eat—and motherly friendliness that made everybody feel better. Emma leaned over the counter before them as they ate, her large arms folded and her pendulous jowls shaking like jelly as she spoke.

"This young lady," she said, gazing knowingly at both of them, "is lendin' an air of respectability to this Sodom and

Gomorrah. Anybody kin see she's been brought up good, and she's made it clear that she ain't goin' to pony up to every Tom, Dick, an' Harry that makes eyes at her." She cast a shrewd look at the girl. "I'm glad to see you two are hittin' it off, 'cuz I think both of you are a cut above what's runnin' the streets in Virginia City."

The girl looked embarrassed. "Well, we're working together, if that's what you mean." She glanced at Warren, and there was no hostility in her gaze.

"This place will get civilized sooner or later," Warren said. "They all do. Right now it's a boom town."

"Well, whatever it is," said Sarah Finley, "I shall do what I think is right and proper, whatever goes on around me."

Don Warren grinned, half at her and half to himself. That primness would be punctured someday. He hoped he would be there to see it.

"Miss Finley and I," he said, "are running the Nancy Belle—together." She glanced at him quickly, without resentment. He laughed. "Maybe the three of us can clean up Virginia City and lift it to higher things."

Emma Nelson shook her large head decisively, and the jowls bobbed and flapped. "Won't never happen while the mines are in bonanza," she said. "When men are makin' money hand over fist, they ain't interested in virtue. If the mines run into borasca, then they'll start prayin', and mebbe there'll be a chanct." Her eyes squinted at Warren. "*Are* they runnin' into borasca? You said you thought they might be, seein' as how none of the big ones would give ye a job."

"I've only been in one drift at the Nancy Belle," he said. "And the vein I saw was getting pretty thin. But the drift boss swore up and down that that same vein widened out into the Lone Star, next door—and the Lone Star already is into bonanza."

"That drift boss," Mrs. Nelson nodded, "that couldn't be Pat Flaherty now, could it?"

"It could," he said. "You know him?"

"Do I know him? The impudent beast! He comes in here all the time and pertends he's int'rested in me."

"He seemed like a nice enough fellow."

She snorted. "It ain't me he's int'rested in. It's the restaurant, as long as it's makin' money. If its profits start goin' down, he'll make himself scarce!"

"Oh, I don't know," Warren said. "You shouldn't be so suspicious. I've only talked to Pat for a few minutes, but he seemed like a right nice person."

"You got to be suspicious in a place like Virginia City," Emma Nelson insisted, wiping off the ketchup bottle and polishing the salt shakers with energy. "You and I," she said to Sarah Finley, "we know, don't we? Us innocent young girls —we got to be real, real careful. Smooth-talkin' gents like this'n"—she nodded at Warren—"an' that Pat Flaherty kin git us into trouble! We got to walk a mighty fine line!"

Sarah Finley ventured a smile at Warren. "Well, I don't know about Pat Flaherty, but I think Mr. Warren is safe enough."

Emma Nelson winked ponderously. "I knowed you two would hit it off! The apple pie's on the house!"

"Oh, I couldn't possibly—" Sarah protested.

"You got to. Otherwise I'll have hurt feelin's. And when a body's as big as I am, there's a lot of feelin's to be hurt. Here!" She placed a thick wedge of juicy apple pie before each of them. "An' I'm goin' to watch you eat it."

"I won't be able to get into my dresses if I do!" the girl said with a sigh. But still she picked up her fork.

It would take more than Emma Nelson's apple pie to ruin Sarah Finley's figure, Warren thought. And with his eyes fixed on her lithe shape, he picked up his own fork.

CHAPTER 4

THE worried-looking male secretary in Belden Ward's office on Montgomery Street opened Ward's door and said, "It's Mr. Cobden to see you, sir."

Ward nodded in response and rose to greet his visitor, who followed the secretary into the inner office. Ward and Cobden shook hands, appraising each other as they did. Cobden was lean, clean-shaven, and bony-featured, with hair graying at the temples. A good two inches taller than Ward, his long, dark coat was equally expensive, his boots shone, and the ring on his finger was of thick gold.

The secretary left the room, and the two seated themselves, Ward behind his large desk, Cobden in a chair facing him.

"You're still interested in selling the Lone Star, I take it?" Ward inquired.

"I wouldn't be here otherwise," said Cobden irritably. "I may as well tell you, Ward, I'm not in agreement with my directors on this sale. We're running into some rich stuff now—eighty and more dollars a ton, and there's a lot of it. I don't think we should sell. But I'm outvoted."

"If that's the case, why do your directors want to?" Ward inquired, taking a cigar out of a silver case and offering one to Cobden, who refused. Ward snipped the cigar's end off with a silver cutter and lit it.

"I'll be honest with you. They think this strike is a final flare-up. They think the Comstock's going into borasca. And there are symptoms: The Mexican, the Gould & Curry, the

43

Ophir—they're not running off at the mouth about it, but they're tightening up, and Bill Sharon's giving signs of concern."

"What about Mackay and Fair and their saloonkeeper partner who're pushing right ahead?"

Cobden nodded. "I see you know what's going on. Mackay and his crowd are convinced the biggest bonanza hasn't even been reached. I'm inclined to agree with 'em. But we've got a lot of nervous Nellies around us, and they've influenced my colleagues."

"How much more of this eighty-dollar ore is there, do you figure?"

"Well, we may be near the end of it because it's bringing us awfully close to the claim line of our next-door neighbor, a small outfit that doesn't amount to much. But it isn't this strike that I'm counting on, and that makes me reluctant to sell. I think the big bonanza's deeper. I agree with Sutro: The real ore is down in the belly of the mountain. But that'll take additional investment, and that's what my partners don't want to risk. As for me, I'm willing to gamble. I don't think Mackay's going to lose, and I don't think we would either—but, as I say, I'm outvoted." He sighed heavily and frowned.

Ward regarded him carefully. If Cobden were putting on a sales act, it was a good one and mighty convincing. Moreover, what he had said, others had said too, about the mines in general. Don Warren had written him twice and had been guardedly optimistic. If Cobden were stretching the truth, it would be about the Lone Star and its strike.

There was one way to find out.

Ward leaned forward and tapped the long ash of his expensive cigar on a silver tray. "Mr. Cobden," he said, "if you mean what you say, and if you've told me a straight story, maybe we can work out something so your directors will be the only losers."

Cobden's face tightened.

"I'm inclined to agree with you," Ward went on, leaning back. "I don't think the Comstock's through—not by a long way! By God, it better not be—with all the money in San Francisco in the Bank of California, and Ralston and Sharon sinking their wad in Sun Mountain! I wouldn't be interested in investing, otherwise. But if I do buy the Lone Star, I'm going to need additional money to dig deeper, and here and now I'm offering you a sizable chunk of that loan if the deal goes through."

Ward puffed smoke at the ceiling and watched Cobden's expression. If there had been the slightest hesitation, the merest tinge of doubt in the man's eyes, he was prepared to drop the whole thing. But there was not. Instead, Cobden's eyes brightened, and he leaned forward excitedly.

"You mean it?" he demanded. "You really mean it?"

"I certainly do. Besides, you know the mine. I'll have to learn it."

"If that's the case," Cobden hurried on, "let's put the deal through! I won't obstruct it. I must admit, I was planning to throw all the roadblocks I could in its way. But with this arrangement . . . and I take it, it's firm . . ." he glanced sharply at Ward.

"I don't break my word," Ward responded stiffly.

"Then let's go forward! Let's talk terms! The price as we discussed?"

Ward nodded and, to prove it, called his secretary.

CHAPTER 5

IT was the following day before Sarah Finley decided what to do with the information Don Warren had given her. Early that morning, just as they both were sitting down at their respective desks, she said, "I think we ought to tell Uncle Grant. But—maybe you shouldn't do it. Maybe I should. If we're wrong, I won't lose my job . . . but you might."

Don Warren listened to that statement with exultation running through every vein and muscle. She didn't want him fired! She had confidence in him! She liked him!

And also, she wasn't sure about her uncle. She suspected that Grant Finley did know about the payoffs.

He rose from his desk and went to her side. "Sarah," he said, "I really appreciate what you've offered. But it won't work."

"Why not?"

"Where would you have learned about it? Did Porter tell you he was making payoffs? No, he told me. I'm the one who's got the books. All you've been doing are wage and production records. Sarah, I really appreciate your generosity, but sooner or later I'd be pulled into it anyway."

"But," she answered slowly, "if he does know it—"

He shrugged. "I'd lose my job." He purposely did not mention what else might happen to him in that difficult town.

"You'd leave—"

He took her hands in his. "Are you implying that you wouldn't like that? That's the nicest thing that's been said to me in a year!"

She pulled her hands away and stiffened. "I—I didn't mean what you think! I was just—"

He laughed happily and went back to his desk. "Don't try to explain," he said. "I'm going to believe what I want to believe! But I should be the one to tell your Uncle Grant. And maybe—just maybe I can figure out a way to do it without getting fired!"

She gave in to him. "How will you do it?" she wondered.

He nodded mysteriously. "Leave it to me! But I want to see him without Porter. First time I can catch your uncle alone—"

They went back to work. It was nearly noon before either of the partners appeared, and, unfortunately, it was Porter. He appeared grumpy and out of sorts, immediately went into his inner office, and slammed the door. The girl turned to Warren. "Uncle Grant must be down in the mine," she whispered. "He goes almost every morning, but today he's staying longer."

Her analysis was correct. Just as the noon whistle of the Gould & Curry screamed its timely blast, Finley entered the office. He still was perspiring from the heat of the lower depths, there was mud on his boots, and his candle cap was on his head, although the flame was blown out. He nodded shortly at the two and disappeared into the inner office, carefully closing the door behind him.

Warren heard a muffled conversation within, followed by louder words which he could not distinguish. The argument subsided, and the low-voiced conversation continued. Finally, as the time neared one o'clock, Finley emerged, scowling. He seemed openly surprised to see Warren and his niece still in the office.

"It's lunchtime," he said. "Don't you two ever knock off?"

"Mr. Porter always tells us when we can go," the girl said.

"Well, I'm telling you today," he barked. "Go on, take your hour. But be back on time. Especially you, Warren. We've got instructions to give you."

Warren glanced knowingly at Sarah, and it led to another generous lunch for the two of them at Emma Nelson's.

"I wonder what he wants to tell you," Sarah mused, pushing aside her half-filled plate.

"Probably something about that drift at the eight-hundred-foot level. They're planning to dig as close as they can to the Lone Star line. I'm supposed to see that it happens."

The minute they finished their lunch, they hurried back to the Nancy Belle, eager to know what the partners had in store for Warren.

He had been correct in his assumption. On their return, Porter motioned for him to come into the inner office, and on his way toward the door, he glanced at Sarah and winked. In return she smiled, somewhat tremulously.

Porter was crouched over his desk, round-shouldered, his cigar at a sharp angle in his mouth. Finley, better groomed and holding himself as erect as his niece, sat at an adjoining desk—a desk, unlike Porter's, completely empty of papers.

"Sit down," Finley invited, waving a bony hand toward a straight chair by the wall. "Like I said I would, I got those figures—and you can go ninety feet farther at the eight-hundred level toward the Lone Star."

Warren pulled the hard chair forward at the same time that he raised his brows. "Won't that take us right into the Lone Star?" he asked. "When I was down there, I could hear 'em digging right through the rock wall."

"That's their funeral," Porter snarled. "Our figures indicate that they already may be over the claim line and into our territory. And if that's the case, there's goin' to be a lawsuit and some excitement."

"Which comes first?" Warren queried. "If we're the ones who break into their drift, I don't see them turning their picks and shovels over to us."

Finley leaned forward. "We'll face that when we come to it—*if* we come to it! There've been wars in the mines before, and they're not much fun, down there in the heat and the dark. But that vein at the eight-hundred level is widening —and we think that ore's ours."

"You *think*?" Warren smiled mirthlessly.

Finley shook his head and looked away. "We *know*," he corrected. "And it's damned important to us. We need every inch of that eighty-dollar ore we can lay our hands on."

"It's your job," Porter added grimly, "to supervise that dig and see that we get all that's a-comin' to us."

"From now on, you're not to spend all your time at your desk," Finley put in. "You're to spend time down below. You're to watch Flaherty. Pat doesn't think my figures are right. He thinks we're already at the claim line."

"Flaherty's pretty experienced, isn't he?"

Finley shook his head vigorously, but again his eyes failed to meet Warren's. "It ain't Flaherty's job to think! It's his job to do what we tell him! And from now on, you're speakin' for us! Now, here are my calculations. Listen to 'em—and then you go to work and get us everything that's rightfully ours!"

Porter took the chewed cigar from his mouth and pointed it at Warren. "This is why we hired you, kid. If you want to keep this job, you'd better get us our share o' that eighty-dollar ore."

Warren held his tongue, telling himself that this was not the time to broach new subjects, even if he could have gotten Finley alone for a moment. Instead, he listened meekly as Finley showed him diagrams and survey data designed to convince him that the Nancy Belle drift at the eight-hundred-foot level could—and should—extend ninety feet farther to the west in the direction of the Lone Star.

Warren listened carefully to the argument. But the more he heard, the more he concluded that the one Finley was trying to convince was himself.

Warren emerged from the inner office to find Sarah Finley waiting for him, almost literally on the edge of her chair.

"Not the right time," he murmured in a low voice as he

passed her desk. "I've got to go below. Maybe this afternoon we can catch your uncle alone."

"Go below? I thought your work was here in the office—"

"They don't call me supervisor for nothing," he smiled wryly. "It's up to me to push a drift ninety feet in a direction the drift boss doesn't think we should go."

"But you're no miner!" she protested. "What could you possibly do below?"

"See that a drift boss follows orders," he explained. "Remember, I'm a supervisor!"

"Oh, be careful," she pleaded—and again Warren felt a surge of exuberance at her interest. He smiled at her and left to change his clothes.

Alone this time, he rode down to the eight-hundred-foot level on the rickety elevator. A candle flickered in a single wall sconce at the entrance to the drift, and he lit his candle cap with it. Then, wearing its light on his head, he carefully made his way into the dark tunnel.

It was different this time. He was by himself. There was no Finley to talk to him and push him companionably on. Pat Flaherty's miners were several hundred feet ahead, and he had only his thoughts for company.

They were not pleasant. He suddenly realized that eight-hundred feet of earth and rock lay above his head, between him and the bright sunshine and the blue Nevada sky. What a business! He had not contemplated this when he had eagerly accepted Belden Ward's assignment to find out more about the Comstock. Well, he was finding out with a vengeance! Directly, not secondhand.

He had donned heavy shoes and, a moment later, was glad that he had, for in one of the darker patches of the tunnel he sloshed through a deep puddle of water. It splashed on his ankles, and he jumped and winced, for the water was hot—as hot as if it had just come off a stove.

The passage suddenly branched into a Y, with a pair of black tunnel entrances looming before him. He halted and cudgeled his brains to remember which one he and Finley had taken on their earlier trip. Why hadn't he asked for more detailed instructions before he came down here?

He made his decision and took the left-hand turn, but within a hundred feet was convinced he had made an error. There were no wall candles here, and the floor of the drift was littered with rocks and earth from the walls. He tripped over a two-foot boulder and fell to his hands and knees, bruising his shin. He uttered an exclamation as his candle cap fell off and the light was extinguished on the ground.

For a long moment he was in utter blackness and in somewhat of a panic. His pulse raced, and he tried to swallow his illogical fear. Deliberately, he took a long breath to calm himself. This was ridiculous, he told himself. Here he was, a supervisor, stumbling around like a frightened child.

He groped for his candle cap. He found the cap, but the candle had bounced away from it—and again a tight grip of fear clutched his throat. He felt frantically around among the rocks and detritus, his discomfort growing by the second, and finally felt—with vast relief—the smooth, waxen surface of the candle as it lay between two rocks. He replaced it in his cap, fumbled for a match, struck it—and once again saw the blessed flickering yellow light before him.

Bathed in cold sweat—sweat which this time was not due to the heat of the drift—he rose somewhat unsteadily to his feet and with great certainty decided that he was in the wrong passage. Cautiously he retraced his steps to the junction of the three drifts, and as he headed into the right-hand earthen corridor, he said a prayer.

This, it seemed, was the right one. The floor was relatively clear of rocks and rubble, and the wall sconces were regularly spaced. In a few moments he heard the sounds of digging ahead, and he made his way to the head of the drift, where once again he saw perspiring miners picking away at the dark vein, sweat glistening on naked shoulders and arms.

Pat Flaherty, huge in the gloom, came up to him and held out a sweaty hand. Like the others he was shirtless, but his Irish skin was white, not tanned, and despite his lean body, before him he bore a memorable paunch, some of it doubtless attributable to Emma Nelson's cooking.

Flaherty grinned. "Glad to see ye. Finley said ye might be comin' along."

Warren shook hands fervently. "You don't know how glad I am to see you!" he exclaimed. "I got in the wrong passage and lost my light. For a couple of minutes I was worried."

Flaherty frowned. "That's bad," he said. "I dunno why they didn't warn ye—I s'pose they thought ye remembered from yer first trip. But that drift's dangerous. Two cave-ins and at the end a pool o' water hot enough to boil chickens. Stay outa that one!"

"From now on I will!" Warren promised. But to himself he reflected that nobody in the Comstock was going to watch out for a loner like him. This was a part of the world where a man had to take care of himself.

"Well, now that ye're here," Flaherty said, "I presume ye're here to carry out Finley's orders."

"You're right," said Warren. "He's figured that this drift ought to go ninety feet farther . . . to see if the vein widens. Isn't that what you're doing?"

The big Irishman frowned. "No, it is not!" he said decisively. "I don't approve of them orders. Finley's as wrong as rain! I seen the survey figgers, and the claim line between us and the Lone Star ain't anywhere's near ninety feet ahead of us! It's closer to twenty. Mebbe even that's stretchin' it a mite! Come here—"

He led the way to the head of the drift and placed his ear next to the rock wall. Warren followed his example and did the same and—as he had on his earlier visit—he heard the unmistakable sounds of digging and labor in the neighboring mine.

"They're not more'n forty feet from us," Flaherty said. "That's Lone Star territory, and we're just askin' for trouble if we break into their drift!"

"Finley says they're over the claim line and are into our territory."

"Finley's crazy as a bedbug!" Flaherty was explosive. He raised a muscular forearm to wipe the sweat from his brow. "Or—" he leaned close to Warren and peered into his face —"maybe he ain't crazy! Maybe he's figgerin' on a little poachin' in Lone Star ore! If he is, he ain't the one who's goin' to do the fightin'—it's us!"

Warren was silent for a long moment. Then he shrugged. "Finley's the boss," he said. "If you haven't been able to convince him he's wrong, I sure can't. What do you mean— fight?"

Flaherty nodded wisely. "There've been wars in the drifts before. And they ain't pleasant. Been a couple cases where miners broke through into somebody else's tunnel, and there's been hell to pay. People killed. These boys"—he nodded at the miners—"are gen'rally good-natured, but they're tough as hell when they're riled. And they rile easy. And Lone Star has the same breed."

"You mean if we break through into their drift, there's liable to be some excitement."

"Liable to be's no word for it! There'll be war—and people hurt!"

"Who owns the Lone Star?"

"Feller named Cobden, Jim Cobden. I don't know him, but people say he's all right."

"Maybe if I had a talk with him—"

"What good'll that do? Ten to one he's got calculations that put the claim line right where we've always thought it was, and that's seventy feet behind where Finley has moved it!"

Warren was silent again, thinking. The miners moved around him, their flickering candle lamps casting eerie moving shadows on the rough walls. The heat was intense. He felt perspiration running down his ribs, down his forehead, and into his eyes. He brushed it away impatiently. The picking, shoveling, and thumping of the miners at the drifthead formed an irritating obbligato.

He took a long breath. "Well, Pat," he said, "I've got my instructions, and I take it you've been told to follow my orders."

"That I have," said Flaherty gravely.

"I'll have to do what Finley told me to do: instruct you to push ahead ninety feet in this drift."

Flaherty shook his head and swore. "It's crazy—and wrong!" he said. "I was hopin' you'd listen to reason—"

"Oh, I've listened to you," Warren assured him. "And I've given you my instructions. I expect you to follow 'em to the letter. But I'll be doing a little looking around myself."

"If that's the case, then so be it," Flaherty grumbled. "But I didn't sign up these boys to be soldiers, an' when we git closer to the Lone Star, I'll want some of 'em to have pistols."

Warren felt uncomfortable. He was reasonably convinced that Flaherty was not exaggerating his concern. "Well, we'll just have to face up to that when we come to it," he told the Irishman, "—if we do."

Still shaking his huge head, Flaherty went back to the vein, which was widening sharply as the drifthead was being pushed farther into the mountain.

As that conversation was taking place at the eight-hundred-foot level, the Panama packet *Darien* was unloading its weary passengers at the Embarcadero dock. One of them was a young man with Don Warren's dark hair and eyes and stubborn chin, and from the deck of the ship he got his first look at the strangeness of San Francisco. What he saw apparently pleased him, for he hoisted his duffel bag to his shoulder, descended the gangplank, and smiled as he set off down the crowded street. It didn't take him long to find his way to the office of Belden Ward.

"You've got to be Don Warren's brother," the proprietor greeted him. "Anybody'd know the two of you were related. You look like him."

"Do I? Well, I guess we must, because others have said so too."

"I'm not surprised. You certainly do resemble him," Warren insisted warmly. "Come on in. Your brother's not here, but

I've promised to help you settle in. You'll feel at home, because you'll be staying in his room."

And so it was that Gregory Warren and Belden Ward made their first acquaintance. The next day—after Greg had written to Don, to inform his brother of his safe arrival—he and Belden Ward had a talk.

"I promised your brother I'd give you a job," Ward began. "And now that I see you, I'm pleased that I did."

"I hope I don't disappoint you, sir."

"What kind of work would you like to do? I've got a warehouse and a mill, and I'm about to invest in a Comstock mine. If you want to stay in San Francisco, I'd suggest the mill. We're short a bookkeeper in the office."

Greg Warren smiled. "I'll do anything you say, sir. But if I really do have a choice, I'd like that Comstock mine. Don's there, and I'd like to be where he is. And everyone's heard of Virginia City. It must be an exciting place!"

"Agreed," said Ward, thinking again how much like Don his brother was. "When the mining deal's completed, I'll find something for you to do. And in the meantime, I don't suppose you'd mind too much rattling around in this Paris of the West."

"No, sir. I sure wouldn't, sir!"

Luck, Greg Warren felt, was clearly on his side, and he left that interview with Belden Ward feeling extremely good. But his smile would not have been as broad if he could have foreseen the dangerous chain of events that his arrival in the Comstock would trigger.

One day passed into another at the Nancy Belle, and somehow Warren never found an opportunity to speak to Grant Finley alone. Porter was almost always in the office before Finley arrived—and usually stayed later than he—and although Virginia City was a small town, Warren never once ran into Finley on the street.

But Warren was learning a great deal about mining—more,

he began to feel, than he really cared to know. Hour upon hour of his time was spent underground in the eight-hundred-foot drift, and more and more effort was required to induce Pat Flaherty to push the tunnel the ninety feet ahead.

"I've had a good reppitation as a minin' man," Flaherty told him. "And I'm not hankerin' to ruin it by poachin' on another's preserves. I'm sayin' right here and now, I'm followin' orders under protest."

Warren grinned. "You've made it clear," he said, tipping his candle cap back on his head so he could wipe the sweat from his face with a blue bandanna, "not only in words, but also by working the men as slow as you can without having 'em take naps during their shift. And that's got to quit!" The smile disappeared from his face. "When I take a job, I do it right. Beginning right here and now, add half a dozen men to each shift. We're gonna push this thing along."

Flaherty shook his head gloomily. "Lone Star's hurryin' too," he grumbled. "And they're a hell of a lot closer than they was. We're goin' to meet 'em damn soon."

"All the more reason to speed up. Come on, now. Let's get cracking! How soon do you figure we'll meet—putting muscle into it, the way we're gonna?"

"A week, maybe two weeks. And I don't want to be here when we do. Remember what I said about issuin' guns to some of the boys—"

"You can't mean that!"

"I sure as hell do!" Flaherty's broad Irish mouth tightened grimly, and he jutted his jaw in the direction of Don Warren's equally stubborn one. "Further'n that, Mr. Supervisor," he sputtered on, "unless we get those guns, I'll order the boys out o' the drift—and I won't go near it, neither!"

Warren stared him in the eye, then—slowly lowering his gaze to the Irishman's white, bulging biceps—remained silent.

The one Warren really wanted to see was James Cobden, owner of the Lone Star mine, but Cobden was in San Francisco and unavailable. So in his place he managed to interview two German immigrants who knew a lot about the Comstock.

One was Philip Deidesheimer. This engineer, sandy-haired with sloping forehead and serious mien, had worked with Cobden in the Lone Star as well as in other mines in Sun Mountain, and Warren sought out Deidesheimer. Warren hoped Deidesheimer might be able to tell him about the mine that appeared to be exploiting the widened vein that had started in the Nancy Belle.

Deidesheimer occupied a small, unpainted wooden office on the slope of Sun Mountain, quite near to one of Sharon's mills, and Deidesheimer was not anxious to see anybody.

"It's important that I see him!" Warren insisted to the mutton-chopped, middle-aged male secretary who guarded the engineer's privacy. "I'm trying to prevent a war in the drifts!"

The stiff-backed man in the rumpled brown European suit held out as long as he could against Warren's insistence. But finally the man gave in. *"Ach, Gott!"* he exclaimed, striking his forehead in a dramatic gesture. *"Jawohl, kommen sie—"*

Deidesheimer was impatient at first, but once he had heard Warren's story, he became interested.

"Ja, that vein iss fery wide in *der* Lone Star. *Und* getting wider!"

"How wide is it?" Warren probed, leaning on the littered desk.

"Twenty . . . thirty feet. It may even go to forty." The engineer smiled his pleasure. "A big—a *gross*—bonanza! *Und* they must use my cribbing!"

Warren had heard of Deidesheimer cribbing. It was a system of fitted timber braces that could be built, cube by cube, into as large an area as a hollowed-out vein required. Already Sun Mountain was literally jacked up with it. As each room-sized deposit of silver was removed, the engineer's cribbing took its place. And Deidesheimer himself was doing well financially, although he seemed more interested in the effective use of his invention than in profits.

Warren cleared his throat. "Where would you say the claim line is between the Nancy Belle and the Lone Star?" he asked unabashedly.

Deidesheimer shrugged. "Dot iss not my business. I haff not examined *der* data. Vot I know iss dot Lone Star iss running into bonanza ore, *und* the farther they drive *der* eight-hundred-foot drift, the bigger the bonanza gets!"

"And they are driving fast?"

"As fast as they can. And vy not? Efery foot brings them thousands of dollars in profits!"

Troubled in mind, Warren rose from his chair. He turned at the door. "Have you ever seen a battle in the mines, Mr. Deidesheimer?"

The engineer shuddered. "Nefer! But I haf heard of such business. Fery bad! I do not vish to be involved in such a violent t'ing."

Warren expressed his profound thanks and left. He had not found out all, but he had found out something. He now knew that the Lone Star *had* hit a bonanza in the same widened vein that the Nancy Belle was exploiting, only at six-inch to one-foot widths. Now he could understand Porter's and Finley's passion to drive ninety feet farther at the eight-hundred-foot level. At the same time he could understand Lone Star's haste to open up their own drift to this bonanza. The maddening thing was that it was the same vein that ran through the Nancy Belle.

He began to feel a genuine sympathy for his bosses, dishonest though they might be. If Pat Flaherty were right, the Nancy Belle had no business driving farther west. But he could appreciate the frustration that came with the realization that Al Porter and Grant Finley could claim a fortune if that claim line had been drawn only a few feet in another directions.

"Go see Sutro!" Pat Flaherty advised. "Sutro knows where our real profits are! He'll tell you we don't have to poach on other fellers' veins to make a fortune. Go see Sutro!"

Warren delayed going for several days, thinking Flaherty's advice was inspired by his antagonism to Finley's data. But with Cobden's continued absence in San Francisco, Warren finally decided to look up Sutro. Any information Warren could get might be helpful.

Reluctantly, Flaherty had increased the size of the drift crew, and the new force was driving forward several feet a day. The Lone Star obviously was doing the same, judging by the sounds and thumps and echoes of dynamite blasts that penetrated the rock barrier. Soon the two crews were bound to meet.

With time tugging at his heels, Warren looked up Adolf Sutro. He was a man everybody knew, and the interesting thing was that he was viewed entirely differently by the miners and their bosses. And there was a reason for it.

Sun Mountain had a lower valley and a higher plateau, and there were hot springs at the lower depths; and also in that area, the possibility of the greatest stores of ore. Sutro knew the Comstock. Like Deidesheimer, he was a German immigrant, and he had visited the mines and had seen the difficulties the boiling water caused. Several mines had had to stop digging for deeper deposits because of it. So Sutro studied the situation and made a plan.

The mines opened onto the eastern slope—and plateau side—of Sun Mountain, and it was Sutro's idea to go to the west side—the lower valley—and drive a tunnel to the east that could drain off the boiling water and permit the exploitation of the vast untapped wealth that he was convinced lay deeper than any the mines had yet probed.

It was this theory that he excitedly elaborated to Warren when the latter found him in his little board office at the foot of the western slope of Sun Mountain. A hundred yards away was a black tunnel-mouth, masonry-lined, leading into the depths of the mountain. Tracks ran from the entrance, and cars full of earth, not ore, rumbled out at intervals. As Warren watched, one work crew emerged from the depths, perspiring, dirt-streaked, laughing loudly, and conversing. Good-natured, they exchanged jokes and insults with the fresh crew, which replaced them in the cars.

Diverted from watching them by the opening of the office door, he saw a portly man with side whiskers, bushy hair, and eager eyes beckoning him to enter. He did so and introduced himself.

Sutro looked him over carefully, shook hands vigorously, and offered him a chair.

"You own a mine, *ja?*" he asked explosively.

Warren laughed. "No, but I work for one. I've got a problem, Mr. Sutro, and my foreman told me you might help me solve it."

Sutro's face broke into a grin. "Your foreman! Then I haf no concern! The miners—they want me to succeed! It iss the owners who oppose!" His face darkened, and he rose and paced the floor excitedly. "The owners! Sharon and Ralston and Mackay and Fair! Because I wish a tiny"—he squinted and held finger and thumb a quarter inch apart—"a tiny profit. Only two dollars per ton. In return for opening up the biggest bonanza efer for them, they fight me and go to Congress to get laws passed to stop me and try to ruin my credit! They are fools! I offer them wealth untold, *und* they fight me!" He shook his head despondently, threw up his hands in a dramatic gesture, and plunked himself down again in his chair, which creaked alarmingly.

"You think there's a lot of ore at greater depths?"

"*Ja!* Certainly! I haf studied mining *und* geology! I haf had advice of experts from Europe! It iss the way silver lies in the earth. Would I spend my entire life and energy to prove it if I did not know it to be true? But you nefer will reach it unless I drain Sun Mountain with my tunnel!" He opened a box of cigars on his desk, selected one, then offered the box to Warren, who refused. "The hot *Wasser*—water—will boil eferyone alive unless I can finish my tunnel! Vy von't they listen?"

"Because you're charging 'em two dollars a ton off the top," Warren said. "They don't like that."

"But those tons nefer will be theirs unless I finish my tunnel!"

"They don't see it that way," Warren told him. "I've only been here a short time, *Herr* Sutro, but I know that some of the owners—not all of them—would rather see miners boiled alive than pay for their safety."

"But they forget that they also would be paying for a bonanza—a bonanza which they will nefer get unless I finish my tunnel!"

Don Warren rose abruptly and held out his hand. "You've told me what I want to know, sir."

Sutro rose, in turn, and took the proffered hand. "*Und* vat is that?"

"That you believe there's a bonanza deeper in the mountain. You've told me it isn't necessary to have a war in the drifts at the eight-hundred-foot level; that we ought to forget that and dig deeper. That's the way I interpret what you've said."

Sutro nodded vehemently, so that his side whiskers bobbed. "*Ja*, I guess so. I *know* there is silver deeper in the mountain, *und* I *know* it nefer will be mined unless I finish my tunnel!" He waved a hand at the open doorway, where the sounds of working men and rumbling cars carrying earth from the tunnelhead echoed loudly. "If there iss a problem at eight-hundred, do not worry! Dig deeper! Deeper, alvays deeper! Zere you will find the ore! But you will not find it without my tunnel!"

Don Warren left his interviews with Deidesheimer and Sutro with a clearer picture of what he had to do. First he went looking for Pat Flaherty.

It was at the eight-hundred-foot level that he encountered him, and Flaherty was grumpily driving his expanded crew forward.

"How close are we?" Warren asked, mopping the sweat from his brow.

"Three or four more days before the breakthrough," the big Irishman replied. "We're not makin' as fast time as Sutro. He's drivin' his tunnel at least ten feet a day, or so I hear."

"We're not yet into Lone Star territory, are we?"

"We sure are!" Flaherty was vehement. "We're well into it, if ye really want to know!"

"Not according to Finley's survey."

Flaherty jabbed a thick forefinger into Warren's chest so hard it hurt. "I keep tellin' ye—Finley's figures ain't worth a damn! He's worked 'em over so they come out the way he wants! And those figures ain't honest! They ain't honest, I tell ye! An' I ain't fightin' in any drift war fer a cause that ain't honest!" He flexed his biceps. "Whin I fight, nobody kin lick me! But Oi'll only fight fer somethin' I believe in. An' I sure don't believe in this!"

"All right, Pat," Warren said. "Hold off. Stop the digging, I say. We shouldn't break our pick at the eight-hundred-foot level if there's a bigger bonanza below." And as the bewildered foreman stood there with his jaw open, Warren told him of his interviews with Deidesheimer and Sutro. "What they say could be true. Let's go deeper!"

Flaherty, instead of responding enthusiastically, as Warren had expected, shook his head and frowned. "If ye kin git the boss men upstairs to go along with ye, it's all right with me. But I doubt it. An' even if ye do, Sutro's tunnel ain't through yet—an' maybe it never will be! An' fu'thermore, now that we've gone this fer, I ain't at all sure I kin stop the bhoys here." He waved a hand at the sweaty miners at the head of the drift. "We're into a four-foot vein, and it's a-widenin' fast! The bhoys are lookin' for another bonanza. There's always a bonus in it fer each of 'em when we strike."

"You can at least try to get them to slow down," Warren advised, scowling. "In view of what I've heard, I don't want a scrap down here where somebody might get hurt. I'm going up now to talk to Porter or Finley—and to both of 'em, preferably."

Flaherty touched his forelock in a mock salute. "Wish ye luck," he said sourly. "But all of me wishes ain't goin' to give it to ye. And mind"—he called after Warren, who already had started for the elevator down the dark, candlelit rock corridor—"whin ye come back, bring the guns I asked fer! When we need 'em, we'll need 'em fast! *I* ain't goin' to be usin' any, but my bhoys will need 'em for defense."

Warren hurried toward the elevator. The cable jerked him sickeningly upward, and suddenly he found himself in bright Nevada sunlight. Walking at a fast clip to the Nancy Belle office, he flashed a smile at Sarah Finley as he passed her desk. He knocked on the door of the inner sanctum.

"Come in," called Porter.

Warren did so, closing the door behind him. He was still in his miner's garb, the candle cap dripping tallow on the floor. He mopped the sweat from his face with his blue bandanna and came to the point.

"You're aware, sir," he addressed Porter, "that there's a big argument about whether we have any right to go any farther toward the Lone Star at the eight-hundred-foot level."

"I know there's been an argument," Porter admitted, impatiently chewing his cigar from one corner of his mouth to the other. "But, hell, our figures are as good as anybody's."

"Whatever the figures are," Warren persisted, "we're facing what Flaherty calls a drift war unless we stop digging right away. Lone Star's shoveling toward us, and we're shoveling toward them, and there's going to be a breakthrough in a couple of days. When it happens, Flaherty predicts trouble."

Porter took the cigar from his mouth and smiled. "And that's when the matter'll be settled!" he declared. "Why do you suppose I wanted you to hurry? I understand we've got a four-foot vein now, and she's widenin' fast. Two more days o' diggin' and we'll likely be in bonanza ore. That's all the time we've got to mobilize our boys for a fight!"

Warren experienced a sinking feeling in his stomach. So this had been the plan! Seizure by force, whatever the legality. "Won't there be a lawsuit?" he asked. "Aren't there some rules to this game?"

"Sure," Porter nodded and leaned back in his creaking chair. "Possession is nine points o' the law! Everybody knows that. But it's hard to draw them claim lines underground. We got one set o' figures; Lone Star's got another. An' after the lawyers have argued their way through a couple sets o' courts, the upshot'll be we'll hold the ground we're on. I'll betcha on it!" Rising from his desk, he jabbed his frayed cigar at Warren. "That's the reason we got to git as far as we can as fast as we can. That's your job, see? Don't muff it!"

"I never signed up for anything like that!"

Porter grew ugly. He thrust his face into Warren's. "Better not drop out on us now, boy! You know the consequences if you show a yellow streak? If your boys lose, they'll take you apart afterward for not leadin' 'em; and if they win, they'll still do it—and with a vengeance! Believe me, I've seen it happen!" He jutted his chin still farther forward, scowling threateningly. "You're there to see we don't lose! You're there to see we hold every inch of ground we've taken. Remember it! If you don't, you'll answer to me as well as the boys!"

The two stood facing each other, immobile for a long moment. Then Warren drew back. "I didn't come here to be intimidated by you, Mr. Porter," he said. "I came to tell you something—something you'll be interested in. I don't like your scare tactics. Don't try 'em on me again!"

Porter pulled his head back into his collar like a turtle, stuck the frayed cigar in the corner of his mouth, and shambled his way back behind the desk. "All right! All right!" he bellowed. "But if you're smart, you'll not forget what I said!"

"I had a talk with Mr. Sutro," Warren proceeded calmly.

"Oh, hell! That crusading nincompoop! He's done more to set the men against their bosses than anybody else on the Comstock!"

"He swears up and down that the biggest ore deposits are deeper. That when his tunnel drains the lower drifts—"

"At two dollars a ton—off the top!" Porter scoffed. "He ain't as dumb as he looks."

"But why go through all this mess with the Lone Star if you can go deeper and find more ore?"

Porter became impatient. "Look, boy, we didn't hire you to

set the policy for this here mine, now did we? Stick to your job. In the first place, Sutro's tunnel ain't finished—"

"But he's close to the Savage. He swears it!"

"Stop listenin' to him, I tell ya! Now where was I?" Flushing red, he took a second to collect his thoughts. "Oh yeah . . . In the second place, we ain't got that kind of time. The Nancy Belle's in hock to Sharon, so to speak, and we need money to pay him back. It's just now gittin' possible. At the eight-hundred level we're comin' into paydirt."

Warren saw no choice at the moment but to retreat and get back to pushing the drifthead in the mine. But that evening, as he emerged from the shaft—grimy, with candle drippings on his shirt—he was thoughtful. Sarah Finley took note of it.

"What's wrong, Don?" she asked sympathetically when they met at Emma Nelson's after Warren had washed up in his room.

He smiled at her. "I don't want to bother you with it, but . . . plenty's wrong!" He leaned forward to tell her, but Emma Nelson had sensed something was wrong and stayed close to listen.

"Any minute we're going to break through into Lone Star," he said, "and I'd bet my bottom dollar there's going to be a fight."

Unable to control herself, the big cook threw her chubby hands into the air and rolled her eyes. "A drift war!" she exclaimed. "My stars and land o' Goshen! I've heerd o' them, an' they're turrible! Down there in the black, usin' picks as weapons, with the candles goin' out an' men fallin' in pools o' boilin' water. Why, Consolidated Virginia had one a couple years ago, an' it was awful! Two men killed, lots of others laid up in the horspital. Don't tell me you're a-gettin' into one!"

"I'm afraid so, ma'am," he confessed. And he went on to tell them of the situation, including his talk with Porter, although he neglected to mention to Emma the question of the validity of the Nancy Belle's claim. Sarah Finley listened to him, aghast. Not that she said much, but Warren saw the concern in her eyes. And at the end of his tale, as the proprietor was picking up the dirty dishes, Sarah reached out a slim hand and placed it over his strong, brown one.

"Don," she said softly, "I'm frightened."

He put his other hand on top of hers and looked her in the eyes. "To tell the truth," he said, "I'm not so calm myself."

In this state of mind he paid their bill, the two of them bade Emma good-bye, and hand in hand they headed toward the boardinghouse where Sarah Finley was staying.

"We've got to talk to your uncle," he told her, "and we've got to talk to him alone. Porter mustn't be part of it."

"I know," she agreed. "But he's hardly ever alone. If he isn't with Porter, he's with someone else. Even if I found him alone, I don't know how I'd bring up the subject."

"Do you know where he is now?"

They were walking down the steep little street that ran off the main thoroughfare, the lights of C Street behind them, the rugged desert hills looming ahead—black silhouettes against a sky which seemed filled with millions of stars. A warm wind blew in their faces, at times so hard they seemed to lean against it.

"There's a light in his room," Sarah said, pointing to a narrow, gaunt, three-story structure which rose before them. "There, on the second floor. But it seems awfully early for him to be in it."

"I think we'd better look and see."

They entered the front hall, which had no rug on the floor and led to boarders' rooms in the rear and, at the very end, to a steep, gray-painted staircase leading to the upper floors. An occasional kerosene lamp on a wall bracket cast shadowed and inadequate light on the stairway.

They began to climb, the stairs creaking eerily and wind whistling around the eaves. Otherwise there seemed to be no life in the boardinghouse.

At Finley's door, they paused and listened. For a moment there was no sound, then they heard a rustling and heavy breathing. Warren raised his hand and knocked.

The rustling ceased. There was a rumbled, "Damn!" and uncertain footsteps came toward the door. It opened, and Sarah's uncle stood before them.

He was disheveled, with a day's growth of black beard on his face beneath the drooping moustache. His eyes were bleary, and he obviously was drunk.

"Uncle Grant—" the girl began.

He shook his head angrily. "You shouldn't be here!" he said. "You oughta be in your room! And you"—he glared at Warren—"what are you doin' keepin' her out all hours?"

"Mr. Finley," said Warren, "we've got to talk to you. It's extremely important."

The tall man waved a careless hand, teetered into a turn, and shuffled away from the door. "Not tonight!" he said. "I don' feel like it. Tomorrow."

Warren could see that the girl was aghast. She had never seen her uncle like this. Just as obviously, this was why he had been so hard to find. Warren suddenly was angry. He took Sarah's hand and pulled her into the room with him.

"Mr. Finley," he said, "we're going to talk. Now! You pull yourself together! We've been trying to get together with you for days, and what we've got to tell you is important."

Finley gazed blearily at the girl. "You shouldn't have come West," he said sadly. "This is no place for you. I'm sorry—"

"Don't be sorry," said Warren. "Just listen!" He took the older man by the arms and forced him backward into a wooden chair that stood by the bed. Finley tried to resist but could not keep his balance.

"Damn you!" he said. "Getcher hands off me—"

"No," said Warren, "I won't. You're going to sit there and listen. Your niece has news for you, and so have I. And we're going to give it to you—straight!"

Finley looked again at the girl, and tears welled in his eyes. "I'm sorry," he repeated. "I shouldn't have let you come."

So there was some real affection there, Warren thought. It was a hopeful sign, unless it was alcoholic in nature. He braced himself to speak.

"I've been going over your books, Mr. Finley," he said, "and somebody's been stealing from you. I told Mr. Porter, and he said he was making payoffs to Sharon for the milling charges." He noted a flickering of Finley's eyes and interpreted it as a gleam of concern. So he stopped. "Did you know about that?" he asked.

Finley took a long breath and straightened himself with an effort. He shook his head as if to brush the haziness from his eyes. "You say—Al's been doin'—*what*?" And again he shook his head. "Tell me!"

"Mr. Porter's been making payoffs to Sharon, sir. That's what he told me."

Finley rapidly was becoming sober. "Payoffs for what?" he demanded. "Why in hell should we be making payoffs? We're paying Sharon through the nose as it is!"

"I don't have the answer to that," Warren responded. "But both Sarah and I wanted to be sure you knew—if you didn't already."

Finley rose to his feet, steadying himself by gripping the back of the chair. His voice was firmer, his gaze clearer. "Well, I didn't! But now I'm beginning to figure out a few things—like why he didn't want you, Sarah, in the office! Afraid you'd find out too much!" He paced the floor of the little room, traces of intoxication rapidly vanishing. Suddenly he pounded a fist into the palm of his hand. "Damn Al! I've left the running of the business to him, and he's been playing games!"

Warren glanced at the girl. Her eyes were riveted on her uncle, her hands clasped so tightly the knuckles were white. He decided to proceed while Finley was receptive.

"One more thing bothers me, Mr. Finley," he said. "The accounts payable jibe with the billings, but they don't match the totals on the balance sheet."

Finley squinted at him. "I don't get you."

"Sharon's bills for milling are all stamped 'Paid.' But the Nancy Belle has spent more for milling than the invoices show. Maybe you can tell me: Are there any other milling charges that would be separate from the milling statement?"

By now Finley was almost cold sober, and he was rapidly getting his mind around the problem. As he thought, he kept running his hand through his hair, as if he were ashamed of his unkempt appearance before his niece. "Not that I know of," he finally answered. "Milling's milling. You hire it done, and you get a bill. Why?"

Warren glanced at Sarah before he spoke, then plunged ahead. "Well, if that extra money isn't going to Sharon, sir—where is it going? Are you and Mr. Porter taking it as part of your salaries?"

Finley eyed him coldly. "You mean am I getting a cut over and above my wages?"

"That could be one way of looking at it."

"Hell, no! And Al keeps telling me we neither one of us oughta be taking out so much!"

Warren was silent for a long moment, and he spent it gazing into Finley's eyes. "Well, somebody is," he said flatly. "And it's a considerable sum. Over the past several months it's run into thousands of dollars."

Finley stood there, still gripping the back of the chair, his face twisting into a scowl. At last he shook off the last of the cobwebs from his brain and swore vehemently.

"Are you telling me Al's been taking a cut?"

"I'm reporting to you what the books show, just the way I reported it to Mr. Porter. If you're partners, both of you should know."

Finley straightened. His voice now was even and he was coldly calm. Not a vestige of his binge remained. "Well, I haven't been *making* payoffs to anybody—or *getting* 'em from anybody!" he declared. "But I'm beginning to understand why we're having trouble meeting our loan commitments." He turned to the girl. "I'm afraid I ain't been a very good uncle to you, Sarah. I've been thinking for quite a while I never should have let you come." Then he turned to Warren. "And from what you've told me, I guess I haven't been a very good businessman. But I'm aiming to fix that before morning!" He reached for his hat on the bureau.

"No, wait!" said Warren. "There's something else you ought to know!"

"I ain't waiting for anything, now that I know this! And you better have told me a straight story, young feller, because I'm taking action!" He thrust past Warren and pushed toward the door.

"Wait!" Sarah pleaded. "Please wait, Uncle Grant! Let Don tell you!" She grasped his sleeve.

His expression softened as he looked down at her. "For you, I'll wait," he said. "But he better spit it out mighty fast!"

"There's going to be a war in the drifts," said Warren without preamble. "We're within a day or two's distance of the Lone Star, and Pat Flaherty wants guns. He's sure the Lone Star's boys feel the same. If they're both armed, there'll be a fight, and people will be hurt!"

Finley dropped his gaze. "What can I do about it?" he asked grumpily.

"Well, Flaherty says we have absolutely no business being where we are, that we're past the claim line. Are we?"

"Not according to my figures." But the voice was low and sullen.

"I can't understand it. If there's a question about it, why should we be drawn into a stupid fracas? Sutro thinks there's a bonanza below us, well within our own claim. Why don't we go after that?"

"I thought the same thing once, and I told Al. But he gave me a lot of reasons why we need money—and fast."

"Didn't we just talk about one of 'em?" Warren asked quietly.

Again a spasm of rage shot across Finley's face. "By God, we sure did! Get out of my way! I'm goin' to see Al now!"

"Now, wait!" Warren cautioned. "We didn't tell you this to have you go off half cocked. Let me ask it again: Are you positive your survey figures are right? Are we within our own claim line?"

Finley's eyes fell, and he looked away from his niece. "They're the best figures I could get," he said lamely.

"Somebody could get killed because of 'em," Warren predicted. "They've got to be right. If they're not—"

He could see that the thing Finley wanted most was to stop talking about the survey. The man clearly preferred to direct his rage at his partner.

"Al talked me into that claim extension!" he grated. "I never did like the idea! And if he's been taking a cut, I'll see to it that we dig deeper if it's the last thing I do. There won't need to be a fight!" Collaring Warren, he said, "Right now I'm ordering you not to push another inch into that drift!" He turned toward the door. "Wait'll I git ahold of that Al!"

They could hold him no longer. Pushing between them, he strode into the hall, clumped down the corridor, and onto the stairs.

"I hope he's not too drunk to handle himself," Warren half mused to Sarah as they watched him go. "But whatever happens, we know he's not involved in whatever monkey business Porter's in."

The girl sighed deeply. "I can't tell you how relieved I am," she said. "He's proved he's not a bad man at all! Just rough and—"

He stopped her words by putting his arm around her shoulders. "For your sake, I'm glad he's not involved," he said. "And I can tell you one thing: I don't envy Porter during the next half hour."

When she did not answer, he looked into her face, and he could tell that she was troubled.

"What's wrong?" he asked. "I think things are heading in the right direction for a change."

"I don't know," she said, and she looked up at him appealingly. "But I have the strangest feeling that—that things may not go right. Mr. Porter can be awfully mean. I'm—I'm afraid for Uncle Grant."

"Oh, pshaw! He can take care of himself."

"But he's been drinking, and—he didn't look well to me, I'm afraid he'll do something rash."

"We can go over to the office to see what's happening."

Warren did not tell her that that was what he had intended to do anyway, except that he had planned to leave her in her room.

They made their way down the stairs and up the dusty road to C Street, then headed toward the looming blackness of Sun Mountain, dotted here and there with lights from the mines. The saloons along the street still were in full swing, with mechanical pianos thumping out tinny melodies, and loud voices and laughter drifting over the batwing doors. As they began the climb to the Nancy Belle, they left the sounds of gaiety and drunkenness behind them.

Warren had been fearful that they might overtake Finley en route. Warren believed that the interview Finley had promised should take place, and he did not intend to interfere with it. His concern proved to be groundless. Finley had moved fast and apparently was already in the little office. There was no sign of him on the path. As they crunched along the dirt in silence, Warren began to analyze the situation in his mind. With the girl's uncle aware of Porter's doings—and not easy in his thinking about the doctored survey—the drift war that Porter had set the scene for could be avoided. The Nancy Belle could do what it should have done in the first place: explore the lower levels, where Sutro was sure another bonanza awaited.

Warren breathed deeply of the warm desert air. He felt immensely relieved. Things were working out all right, after all.

A shot sounded from the direction of the little office.

Warren and the girl halted in their tracks and stared at each other. She placed a hand over her mouth. "Oh, no!" she cried.

They set out at a run up the steep slope.

Breathless, they arrived at the shacky little building. The yellow light still glowed through the window. Warren burst through the doorway, the girl at his heels. The outer office was empty, but the door to the inner one was open. Warren reached the doorway and immediately turned to prevent Sarah from entering. But it was too late. The two stood at the doorway and gazed, shocked, at the scene within.

Porter's chair had been overturned. He still lay in it, in an awkward position, with his head propped up by the wall and his legs over the upset chair. He held a smoking, long-barreled Colt in his hand, and he swung the muzzle toward the two as they entered.

Neither paid any attention to Porter or the gun. Both were looking down at Finley, who lay on his back, his mouth and eyes open, with blood welling from a spot in the center of his chest.

"Uncle Grant!" the girl screamed. But Warren held her back. Finley's eyes were unseeing. Porter had shot him squarely through the heart.

As they stared in disbelief, Porter struggled to free himself from the overturned chair. His shirt was torn, and there was a bruise under his left eye which was rapidly turning blue. After he had regained his feet, he watched the two warily, the gun still in his hand.

"What the hell have you done?" Warren demanded.

"He came in here fightin' mad. Before I could even get out from behind my desk, he tried to beat me up! Don't you see?" Porter said. "I had to shoot him. He'd have killed me!"

The three stood there, Porter still panting, the acrid odor of gunsmoke in the air, the girl sobbing softly, her hands clenched at her cheeks.

CHAPTER 6

SLEEP was not in the picture that night for either Warren or the girl. First, there was the conversation with the marshal, who seemed disposed to accept Porter's story of self-defense, and in any case took the matter lightly. Killings were not unusual in Washoe, and quarrels between business partners were common. For the life of him, Warren could not believe the marshal's nonchalance, but what Warren was thinking had little effect. He had to decide whether to stay. But first he had to find an undertaker, and it took him until around midnight to locate one—a tired oldster who grumblingly took charge but made no bones about his resentment at being awakened. It took a little while to make the arrangements, but once they were taken care of, Warren turned instinctively to the girl, who by now was pale and silent, and extended his arm to walk her to her boardinghouse.

At the door to her room she broke down. "I'm never going back to the Nancy Belle," she cried, wiping tears from her eyes. "So how am I going to get the things in my desk?"

He wanted to grab her in his arms and hold her close. Instead, he put both his arms on her shoulders and looked into her eyes. "You're not giving me credit for being even half a friend," he told her. "I'll pick up whatever you want and bring it to you tomorrow night at Emma Nelson's."

"You're not going back there to work!" Her horror showed.

He moved away from her. "I'm going to put Porter behind bars!" he said, staring without seeing into space. "I'm going to

74

study those books until I'm blue in the face, and when I'm through, I'll have enough evidence to prove the accusation I'm going to make. Then they'll not look at the murder of your uncle so lightly! They'll know why Porter wanted him killed!"

"Oh, Don," she said, "I'm so afraid. Porter may try the same thing against you. He wants you to hold that drift against the Lone Star, and when they break through, that can mean fighting. Holding that tunnel's not worth getting killed!"

"Maybe what happened tonight will slow things down," he philosophized. "I hope so. But whatever happens"—and again his eyes glazed and he stared into the distance—"I'm not walking out of that place until Porter gets what's coming to him. I wouldn't dare! He'll destroy the books!" The grim look left his face, and he took her hand and put it in his. "Have you thought about what you're going to do, Sarah?" he asked softly.

"I don't know," she answered truthfully. "Uncle Grant was my only living relative, and I never would have come to a place like this if it hadn't been for him. Now I have nobody."

"Yes, you have," he answered. "You've got me."

She smiled through a tear. "But you might get hurt. Why don't you quit the Nancy Belle?"

Again his thoughts seemed someplace else.

"Have you thought," he said quietly, "that you may now be half owner of the Nancy Belle?"

Her eyes flew open.

"It's quite possible, if you and your uncle are the only living members of your family. It would be foolish for you to let Porter walk away with the whole thing."

"Why, it's never crossed my mind. Do you think there's a will?"

"There could be. Tomorrow, after you've rested up, look through the things here in his room. And I'll go back to the office right now and go through his desk. Porter'll think of it—if he hasn't already."

She clutched his hand, and he suddenly realized that he had

been holding hers all the while they talked. "You've got to be careful!" she urged. "*Please* be careful!"

But Porter was not in the office when Warren returned to the mine. All was dark. Dawn, in fact, was just beginning to brighten the sky to the east when Warren relit the lamp hanging on a chain from the ceiling and started his search of Finley's desk.

There was not much in it. Finley was the hard-rock miner, not the businessman who kept the records. There were back issues of mining journals with articles underlined, one even about Deidesheimer cribbing and another on Sutro and his project. And there were business letters and an important-looking document which turned out to be a copy of the partnership agreement between Porter and himself.

Warren was turning its pages when footsteps clumped into the outer office, and as he listened, Porter—looking somewhat the worse for wear, the bruise under his eye now large and black, and without his customary unlit cigar—strode into the doorway.

He stopped short at the sight of Warren. "What are you doing here, kid?" he asked. And before Warren could answer, he ordered, "Get out of this office!"

"Miss Finley's asked me to bring her her uncle's things," he said evenly. But as he said it, he rose and stood with his hands at the ready.

"The business records of the Nancy Belle don't belong to Finley," Porter flared. "They belong to the mine."

"And Miss Finley now is co-owner of the mine, if I understand your partnership agreement," he said, gesturing boldly with the document he held in his hand.

Porter flushed an angry red. "If Grant didn't leave a will, his share goes to the surviving partner. And you ain't got no will!"

"That isn't the way I read this agreement," Warren replied coolly. He had not had time to read through the whole thing, and he hoped desperately that Porter was bluffing and that he had interpreted the situation correctly.

Porter seemed nonplussed. "You git out of this office and git to work!" he barked, returning to the theme with which he had started the conversation. "Lone Star might break through into the Nancy Belle this very day—and if you want to keep your job, you'd better be ready to handle it!"

Warren said no more, but folded the copy of the partnership agreement, put it in his pocket, and left the office. At least Porter was not going to fire him, he thought. But later, when he ran it through his mind, he realized he should have thought about it sooner.

In spite of all that had happened, it still was too early for the eight-o'clock whistle, and as he hurried back to the boardinghouse to hand-deliver to Sarah Finley the document he had found, he read it, word for word. He was relieved to discover that there was no provision for the surviving partner to assume the entire holding. It was strange that it was treated so summarily, he reflected. But he was glad that it was. It meant there would be a good legal claim for Finley's only relative to inherit his half of the mine, even if she were not his daughter.

He climbed the stairs and burst into the room where he had left the girl. She was sitting on the edge of the bed, weeping, dressed exactly as he had left her. "Did you find a will?" he asked gently.

She looked up at him tearfully. "I just can't bear to look through his things," she said.

He sat down by her side. It had been a rough time for her, he realized. Even while Finley was alive, she had been uncomfortable in Virginia City. Now, shocked by the horror of his tragic death, she was completely shattered by the violence.

He put his arm around her. "Look," he said, "I know it's hard, but try not to worry. We'll put this room under lock and key, and tonight I'll help you look through your uncle's papers. He may not have any, you know. There's always that chance. But I've got one here for you, for sure!" And he pulled the folded mining agreement from his pocket and handed it to her. "Hang onto it with all your might!" he said. "Porter's already trying to twist its contents to his advantage." He turned her head to face him squarely. He still saw that perfect oval, despite the tear-stained face. He smiled into her eyes. "Try to get some rest!" he ordered. "Tonight, after we've had some of Emma's home cooking, we'll search together for your uncle's will—and if there *is* one, we'll find it! After all," he said lightly, "you may be the wealthy owner of a mine. And now that I'm in the same business, I'm not going to desert you!"

Her sobbing quieted, and she seemed to want his arm to stay where it was. But the morning whistles from the slope of Sun Mountain began to sound, one after the other shrieking their call to the hard-rock men. He rose. "I've got to go," he said, "or I'll lose my job—and I don't want to have that happen until your claim to half of the Nancy Belle is firm and clear!"

She clutched his hand. "Don't go!" she begged. "I can't stand the thought of you down in that mine—"

"I don't want to go either," he said—and meant it. "But I've got to watch Porter. He'll try some shenanigans if I don't, and I'm bound to see that you come out of this all right."

He left her reluctantly and ran back down C Street to the mountain slope and the mine.

Porter was waiting for him at the office door.

"You git below!" he ordered angrily. "They're close to a breakthrough! You be there and hold onto every foot! Don't go hangin' back, see! Push your way into their drift!"

Warren snatched his miner's cap, thick with candle grease, from the hook above his desk and ran to the elevator, which already was full of the dozen men of the first shift. He gripped the pipe handbar, and his last look was of Porter, glaring at him, as the bottom dropped out of his world and the elevator carried him and the other twelve down the dark shaft to the eight-hundred-foot level.

PART 2

CHAPTER 7

IN San Francisco the preceding afternoon, Belden Ward sent a message to his mill near North Beach. Addressed to Gregory Warren, Esq., it read:

Dear Greg,

At the Comstock, Lone Star and a mine next door are having a squabble about boundaries. They're digging toward each other, and when thy break through, there's liable to be quite an argument.

If you want excitement, this is it. Leave for Virginia City right away. Go to Lone Star Mine, and ask for Jim Cobden. The enclosed note is for him, and tells him that I am sending you. Protect my interests. The important thing is to make sure Cobden lives up to his agreement.

Yours faithfully,

/s/ Belden Ward

Greg Warren read the note at the stand-up desk where he had been working for two weeks. He smiled. Great news! Now he could see his brother and the excitement at Washoe. No answer had come as yet to his letter to Don, and while it was not surprising, considering the slowness of the pack-mule mail express, his eagerness to see his brother was mounting.

He showed the note to his boss, cleaned up his desk, finished the job he was working on, and left Ward's mill for good. He went to his room, packed his few necessities in a worn carpetbag, the same one he had carried from New Orleans and across Panama. He paid his fare on the Morgan Stage Line to Sacramento, where, he was informed, he would have to leave the Concord and transfer to a lighter mud-wagon for the climb over the Sierra.

The little ferry left next morning at six, and three hours later Greg found himself on the east side of the Bay, in a shiny Concord coach, jammed in the front seat, riding backward, with a sour-faced, heavyset woman clad in stiff and rustling black, and a miner in corduroys and red shirt as his seatmates. Facing him were three other passengers on the jump seat, constrained and uncomfortable. Two of them were businessmen in somber garb and one was a pretty, hard-faced girl in a ruffly, mustard-colored traveling outfit and a plush purple hat with a large brown ostrich-plume adorning it. She wore cheap, flashy jewelry, and Greg concluded that she was one of the painted women he had heard about, going to take a job in one of the dens of iniquity that, he was sure, abounded in Virginia City.

Back of them sat three other passengers in the rear seat of the Concord, also facing him over the shoulders of the businessmen and the girl. One of these wore a derby with an ivory toothpick in its band, a suit with large brown and yellow checks, spats, and had a waxed and curled moustache and a leering expression—and Greg felt he must be a drummer on his rounds. The other two were a middle-aged married couple, and Greg suspected they were going to the mountain of silver to start a business and, hopefully, make their fortune.

That trip over Donner Pass to the silver country was an exciting experience for the boy from Ohio. He had felt that nothing could be more interesting than the journey by paddle-wheel steamer to the Isthmus, the trek through the jungle to the Pacific side, then the rough and crowded boat trip to San Francisco. But the stage ride changed his opinion.

The six horses drew the Concord at a gallop up the east side of the Bay, then cut over to the Straits of Carquinez, where the passengers alighted from the coach, took a rowboat ferry to the other shore, and jammed themselves in another, much older Concord. The coach started out again as the laboring horses, snorting and snuffling, drew the heavily laden vehicle up the slopes of the coast range, through yellow-brown hills dotted with live oak, and down a shorter grade into a valley so flat and vast that Greg was certain there was no end to it.

On the sprawling flats the six horses resumed a gallop, and the Concord rattled and bounced dustily toward Sacramento, rolling forward and back on its leather thoroughbraces like a ship at sea.

The sun was high now, and it blazed and burned downward as if fed by the fires of Gehenna. Even the breeze caused by the Concord's passage was hot as from a furnace. None of the men in the coach, although they were perspiring freely and large patches of sweat soaked through their clothing, dared to remove their coats in the presence of ladies. The ladies themselves, swathed in yards of material, were perspiring delicately, with the exception of the heavyset woman by Greg's side, who emitted odors so muscular that Greg was certain she had not bathed in a month.

The drummer with the waxed moustache could maintain silence for a short time only, and long before the stage coach had dropped down into the Sacramento Valley he had struck up a conversation with the married couple on his right and was attempting one with the hoyden on the center seat. Greg watched and listened with amusement. The large woman by his side had not uttered a word since the journey started, and she glared with obvious disapproval upon the conversational gambits of others. The miner dozed, despite the bumps and lurches, and the major problem facing Greg was having to stare into the three faces opposite him on the jump seat.

The coach changed horses every twelve or fifteen miles, at tiny stage stations, often not more than sheds on the plain. At one of them, shortly after noon, the passengers were invited to alight and partake of lunch in a tiny adjoining saloon. Slabs of tough beef between slices of brown bread, coffee, and—if you wanted it—whiskey comprised the bill of fare.

But despite the discomforts, the beauty and impressiveness of the land kept Greg fascinated and less conscious of his troubles. The live oak in the hills, with black patches of shadow under them; the Spanish broom, purple sage, and aromatic greasewood on the plain; the pale green rustling cottonwoods by the banks of streams and dry channels—all made the land one of strange and lonely beauty. A huge, dark bird circling alone in the empyrean attracted his attention. The miner noted his interest and roused himself briefly to remark, "Condor. Biggest bird in the world."

Deer started out of brush by the side of the road and just made it across before the stage rattled by. Once the miner nudged him and pointed as a shambling brown body vanished in a clump of brush.

"Bear," he said. "Dangerous sons-o'-bitches. They look friendly but they ain't. And they're always hungry."

Then the country grew lower, with patches of swamp and marshland, and shortly after dark the stage, with its last change of horses, arrived in Sacramento.

Sacramento was a bustling, dusty, board-and-batten, tent-roofed river port to the mines. The stage, which had been lumbering along, speeded up as it entered town, and the driver, with a flourish for all to see, drew up before an unpainted office bearing the sign, *Morgan Stage Lines* on its false front. The driver, whom everyone called the Whip, announced in stentorian tones, "All out! Sacramento! Those goin' on will wait here for the next coach! You kin git a drink in the bar next door."

Favoring stiffened joints, the passengers from San Francisco climbed from the Concord with some difficulty and no little relief and entered the crowded, hot little office.

Greg went to the counter. "I'm going to Washoe," he said.

The officious personage behind the counter said flatly, "Stage is late. Comin' in from Grass Valley. You got an hour or more to kill."

Greg sighed and entered the saloon-cafe adjoining.

"Lissen," said the drummer with the checked suit and

derby, who by now was standing at the bar, "you look like a sport to me. That babe with the ostrich feather—look she's sittin'over there—she's just waitin' for attention from some respectable gents like us. Why don't we go overand try to git a little frien'ly so we don't have such a dull trip over the hill?

Greg looked at him. "Since when has that sort of thing been a partnership deal? Why don't you go over yourself if you're interested?"

The drummer put down his glass, which at that early hour had been refilled more than once. "I already made up to her," he explained. "An' she's playin' hard to get. I figger if two of us make the approach, she'll have a hard time turnin' us down. An' if she is willin' to git friendly, I'll take over if you ain't int'rested." He looked Greg up and down—the straight-featured face, the honest eyes, the neat, inexpensive clothing. "If you're with me, she'll have a hard time turnin' us down," he repeated.

Greg looked away. "You're on your own," he said and laughed.

"No, please!" the man said. "Walk over there with me anyhow! She won't even give me a tumble, and you're a nice-lookin' gent. You'll help me break the ice. C'mon, be a sport!"

Greg shrugged. "All right," he said. "Let's go. But remember, she's all yours."

"Bartender!" the drummer shouted, pounding the bar. "One more li'l snort!" He turned back to Greg. "Got to oil the works. Gives me a gift of gab."

"I don't think you need it." Greg smiled. "If you want to make a pitch, let's get on with it. I want to look around town before the next stage comes."

The two approached the table where the pretty, hard-faced girl with the purple hat and ostrich plume sat sedately sipping a beer.

The drummer sashayed up with aplomb, removed his bowler, and managed a sweeping bow. "Miss," he said, "I failed to introduce myself properly when we spoke before. My name is Ed Musgrove, and this here is—" he waved a hand at Greg and regarded him quizzically.

The girl raised arrogant brows and lifted her upturned nôse still farther. "*We* didn't speak, " she said loftily in a harsh, unmusical voice. "*You* accosted *me*—a woman alone, which I hardly think is proper. However her gaze softened as she looked at Greg—"your friend seems to have more proper manners when travelin' in mixed company, and I'd be pleased, I'm sure, to meet him." She held out a gloved hand in the manner of a queen offering her hand to kiss. Greg, secretly amused, took the tips of her fingers and bowed over them in stately fashion.

"My name, Miss, is Gregory Warren. And yours?"

She smiled as he took her hand, and her eyes softened to butter. "Birdie Boynton," she said. "*Miss* Birdie Boynton. I'm headin' for Virginia City, where I expect to find suitable employment."

Musgrove moved in. "Now me," he said, "I'm doin' the same thing—headin' for Washoe. But I've already got employment. I'm travelin' in sewin' kits. I'll be glad to show you one when I git back to my luggage."

She ignored him. "Mr. Warren," she interrupted, "you look like *such* a successful businessman. If I'm not too bold, might I ask about *your* business?" She simpered prettily and batted her mascaraed lashes.

Greg smiled at her, and his conquest was complete. "I'm in mining, ma'am."

She was won. She rose and took his hand in her gloved ones. "Mining!" she squealed. "*Such* a romantic callin'! And in Virginia City! I understand that's where the money is."

"Well, there are a lot of other people makin' money too," Mr. Musgrove put in, edging closer.

The girl turned her back to him and continued to concentrate on Greg.

"I say," said Musgrove, "we three oughta sit together goin' over the pass. We could have a frien'ly time of it."

It was as if he were not among the living. Miss Birdie Boynton addressed herself to Greg completely, and as she moved closer and Greg inched backward, Mr. Musgrove found the distance between them increasing. He stepped forward. "Now, looka here," he said. "*I* was the one engineered this intraduction, and—"

She cast a cold glance over her shoulder. "A *gentleman* does not accost an unescorted lady without an introduction. And as I recall, sir, we have never been introduced!"

"Well, maybe I can remedy that," said Greg somewhat desperately.

But the girl interrupted with several paragraphs of chatter that one reason she was going to the Comstock was she always had been *fascinated* by minin', and she hoped they could sit together on the next stage so he could tell her *all* about it.

"I don't know much about it," said Greg. "I'm just starting—"

She took him by the elbow and steered him toward the door, away from Mr. Musgrove, chattering gaily, while Mr. Musgrove, bowler in hand, scowled at them helplessly.

That nocturnal journey over the Sierra was an experience Greg always would remember. Later, when he thought of it, he recalled the darkness, with a stage-bright moon rising in a star-filled sky; the odor of sage and greasewood and, at the crest, the towering pines; the thumping, bumping, clattering, lurching mud-wagon, its leather curtains rolled up and flapping noisily against the frame; stage stops where the horses were quickly and expertly changed in sheds hidden by first brush and then the pine forest; the summit of the pass, where the road suddenly leveled out by the side of a silent, mysterious, glass-smooth lake.

The old miner still was riding backward, but Greg now was in the jump seat, with Birdie Boynton between him and Musgrove. The miner leaned forward. "Donner Lake," he said, and for a moment the girl quieted and permitted a lull in her ceaseless conversation. "That," said the old man, "is where a bunch of immigrants got snowed in and ran out of food and et each other."

Greg almost shivered. This scene suddenly was grim and menacing—unlike the friendly, brush-clad slopes and the soft pine forests. It was almost as if the tragedy of that terrible journey and the sins of that place had cast a pall over the mountain valley. Even the girl seemed subdued, and it was a few moments before she resumed her stream of talk.

After some hours Greg had become inured to the talk. It had bothered him at first, and he had done his best to bring Musgrove into the conversation. But it was fruitless. The girl had eyes only for Greg, and when the drummer attempted to join in, she snubbed him rudely.

Shortly after one o'clock in the morning, after they had halted for a midnight snack at a stage station high in the mountains, the conversation began to lag, much to Greg's relief. First, the old miner's chin dropped on his chest and he began to snore. Then the drummer took off his derby and competed in noisy slumber. And at last, even the girl began to nod. At times all of them were jerked awake by the lurches and thumps of the mud-wagon, but despite this, all fell into a broken, uncomfortable doze.

Greg was the last to drowse off. He was too excited about the trip; about the massive, moonlit scenery and the risky dirt road the rattling mud-wagon careened over at reckless speed. Finally, however, as the stage came out of the Sierra and descended the rolling foothills, he fell asleep. Later he awoke with the bright morning sun shining in his eyes and the Whip shouting, "All out fer breakfast!"

They had thick flapjacks and coffee in a hot little shed, then reentered the stage, and shortly before noon entered Virginia City.

There, Greg knew, was the mountain of silver, its dry slopes dotted with mines and smelters and smoke-belching stacks. There was the wildest town in America, full of money and sin. There also was his brother.

CHAPTER 8

At the eight-hundred-foot level, Don Warren—in wax-stiffened miner's cap and rough, riveted canvas pants—sought out Flaherty. The big Irishman emerged from the shadows at the drifthead, his face somber.

"We're gittin' closer," he warned. "Where are them guns I ordered? The boys are skittish. They know their friends on the other side o' that rock wall are armed to the teeth and will come in shootin' when they break through. Porter wants our men to fight, and they're willin'—but he's too damn tight to arm' em! Why the hell is he so slow with them guns?"

Warren looked into the big, red, pug-nosed honest face, dripping with sweat, streaked with dirt. "Pat," he said, "I have something to tell you. Come back out of earshot with me. It's not for the others."

In the darkness of the tunnel, with the light from a wall sconce flickering yellowly on their shadowed features, the sound of picks and dripping water in their ears, Don Warren told the foreman of Finley's death and of his suspicions of Porter.

Flaherty removed his hat and scratched his reddish thatch. "Begorrah!" he exclaimed. "An' it would have to be Finley, the only one o' them two who knew anythin' about minin' and was himself half a human bein'!" He shook his head despondently, then lifted his eyes to face Warren's. "Then we don't hafta push this drift no farther!" he exclaimed. "We're into Lone Star's territory already—I know damn well we are! We can quit, and when Lone Star breaks through, we'll hold the ground we got! But sittin' here quiet-like, just as if it was ours, there'll be damn little blood on the floor. Only if we keep on diggin' like mad and face 'em through a hole in that wall can there be big trouble. Now" he said and grinned slowly "we don't hafta!"

The thumping picks of the miners at the drifthead came to them, along with a muffled boom from a distant subterranean blast. A further consequence was a shower of powdery dust as the earth shook from the dynamite. The yellow light flickered on their faces.

"You look as though you got somethin' else to tell me," Flaherty said.

Warren scowled. "It's nothing definite," he said. "Just something I *think* is going to happen."

"Well, what is it?"

"That Porter's going to force us to take every inch of that vein we can—and that he's going to try to swindle Finley's niece out of her share of the Nancy Belle, make a big killing, and then leave or sell out."

Flaherty shrugged his big shoulders. "How can he force us?" he asked. "What can he do?"

The answer came to them as if deliberately timed. The faraway rumble of the shaft lift had reached their ears moments before, and now they heard running feet approach. Down the dark corridor of the drift, flickering miners' cap lights first bobbed into sight, then came rapidly toward them. In a moment Porter was discernible, with three men.

Porter, for a change, had substituted a short-barreled shotgun for his cigar. Of the three with him, Warren did not recognize any as employees of the Nancy Belle, but all were similarly armed. The surviving partner lost no time coming directly to where Warren and Flaherty were standing.

"Why ain't you over there pushin' your men?" he demanded. "They're workin' like they was half asleep! Soldierin' on the job, they is! If you two got any idea of slackin' off on this vein, you got another think comin'. Now git over there and force 'em to work!" He brandished the shotgun for added effect.

Warren and Flaherty looked at each other. "Mr. Porter," Warren broke in, "Mr. Finley instructed us to stop digging here—'cause his figures weren't accurate," he said. "We're already in Lone Star's claim."

Perspiration rolled down Porter's forehead and into his eyes—eyes which were popping with determination and rage. "Finley's dead!" he shouted. "I'm the sole owner o' the Nancy Belle—an' don't you forget it! Now git over there and do what I told you!" He rammed the twin muzzles of the shotgun into Warren's stomach "So help me, I'll blow a hole right through you."

Warren winced with pain from the pressure of the weapon, and Flaherty shook his head in defeat. "C'mon, kid," he said. "We're outgunned. Let's go."

Reluctantly the two moved to the drifthead and ordered the miners under them to speed their pace. Not trusting to chance, Porter stood close behind them, shotgun at the ready. And the three henchmen with him moved into position to cover the rest of the work crew, who saw the problem and labored faster under the threat, casting nervous eyes over their shoulders.

The picks moved faster, sweat rolled off the brows and shoulders of the men, muffled blasts from distant drifts rumbled through the mountain, and the sounds of the Lone Star's miners on the opposite side of the thinning rock barrier grew louder.

"You two pitch in!" Porter shouted to Flaherty and Warren. "Pick up shovels and git to work!" And seeing his shotgun pointed in their direction, they did.

Shoveling the rock into the cart as fast as the miners could pick it from the vein—in 120-degree heat, with scalding water dripping from underground springs down the sides of the tunnel—was as hard and unpleasant a labor as Don Warren had ever done. Young and strong as he was, the heat, humidity, and bad air made his head swim. Yet every time he slowed his pace, he heard Porter's rasping voice behind him, urging him on.

And from the other side of the rock wall, the sounds of digging were coming closer.

Resisting the impulse to rush first to see his brother, Greg Warren dutifully asked about the whereabouts of Jim Cobden. He was directed to Sun Mountain, to a small, unpainted building on the slope next to a shed housing a steam donkey and an elevator frame.

This must be a deep one, he thought, if the mine is reachable from the surface only by way of a vertical shaft. He shrugged. He had never been down in a mine before, and he was hoping he would like the experience. Many were the stories he had heard about the Comstock drifts, with their terrible heat and rivers of hot water, cave-ins and bad air, so he was forewarned that all might not be pleasant.

He knocked on the door of the office. A male secretary opened it and asked him his business.

"Belden Ward sent me," he said. "I've come a long way to see Mr. Cobden."

"He's inside."

The man jerked a thumb at a corner desk, where a tall, square-shouldered, clean-shaven man sat bent over account books.

Greg approached him. "Mr. Cobden?"

The man looked up. He had hard blue eyes, and his gaze was direct and exploratory. He wasted no words but looked his question.

"I'm Greg Warren. I'm carrying a letter to you from Mr. Ward in San Francisco."

Cobden relaxed slightly and reached for the letter. He read it carefully, then looked Greg up and down. "Ward tells me you're looking for excitement."

"I might be."

"Well, we'll have some shortly. Mine next door's moving into our territory and we're digging toward each other at eight hundred feet. There's going to be a breakthrough, and the gang down there are all hard-rock men. They need someone with brains to tell 'em what to do. Ward says you got the brains. You want to lead 'em?"

"Tell me more."

"We've got to defend our rights. My men are armed. So are they. When they break through, we want to push 'em out of the part of the vein they've already encroached on. There could be shooting. Usually not. Usually just fist fights and pick handles. If you're smart and handle it right, we might get ours back without any trouble. Are you on?"

Cobden had spit it all out, trusting to his gut instinct in judging character. In Greg Warren he saw the right man for the job.

Greg hesitated. "I might be able to work it out—but first I'd have to know more. You say there's an argument about the claim line?"

Cobden regarded him sharply and smiled. "Ward's right. You are smart!" And with that he pulled a roll of blueprints from a shelf and unfurled them on his desk.

The two bent over them as Cobden made his case.

The office door slammed open. A corpulent, sweaty man stood before them, his miner's candle cap askew, his hair mussed. And his clothes covered with rock dust.

The secretary, who had been bypassed by the forcible entry, stood aside nervously.

"Well, I'm here," the man announced. "What do you want?"

Cobden rose to his feet. "Well, if it isn't Al Porter!" he greeted. "I never would have believed you could come so fast!"

He turned back to Greg, waving at the same time to his secretary. "Perkins will take you over to the elevator. Go to the eight-hundred level. Meet the drift boss. His name is Ben Steele. See what's going on. Then come back and tell me what you think."

He hustled Greg through the doorway and waved Porter into the recently vacated chair.

"You look as though you'd been down below," Cobden began.

"Yeah. We're tryin' to git as far forward as we can before the breakthrough. Why in hell would you want to interrupt me?"

"I hear something happened to your partner."

If Porter was startled by the directness of the remark, it was not visible in his manner.

"Right!" he answered unhurriedly. "Finley came into my office fightin' drunk, and I had to shoot him or he'd have killed me. Has that got somethin' to do with you?"

For a long moment Cobden studied him. "You always did look like more of a reasonable cuss to me than Finley. Maybe that's what's got to do with it. Anyhow, guess you can spare a minute away from the mine to hear what I'm going to tell you."

"I'm here. Spit it out!"

"I'm selling out to Belden Ward."

"The Frisco tycoon? That's funny. I just hired a young feller who worked for him."

"Let me put it another way," Cobden continued. "If I weren't selling out, I wouldn't be talking to you. I'd be down there fighting for every inch."

"You're not telling me you've given up?"

"To the contrary. I've got a better deal in mind. That's why I'm telling you. As I say, you've always looked like a reasonable cuss—"

He leaned back in his chair and looked sharply into Porter's eyes—"I know that you know you're moving into Lone Star territory at the eight-hundred level."

Porter stiffened. "Damn if we are! Just before he died,

Finley recalculated the boundary from the same survey we both used, and—"

"You know damn well you're in our territory—and on the basis of that survey. Finley must have juggled the figures."

Porter reddened and stood up. "I don't have to take that kinda talk—"

"Oh, sit down and cool off!" Cobden said and grinned. "I didn't get you over here to call you a crook. But you know good and well that on the basis of that survey—the same one we both used—Finley's recalculations won't hold water." He leaned forward and fixed Porter with a penetrating gaze. "What if I told you the survey's wrong—and maybe Finley's right?"

Porter gazed in surprise at his host. "What are you gittin' at?"

"What if I told you the surveyor had been paid off, and the four-foot vein Lone Star's getting into is really yours?"

"Are you tellin' me the survey we both used was fixed?"

Cobden cleared his throat. "You catch on quick. But my telling you won't do a damn bit of good if it gets in court, because I'll deny it if it gets that far and make you look like a fool—a crooked one. There is a way, though. How would you like to get hold of a couple of letters from that surveyor in which he admits the survey's crooked and asks for his payoff? I did pay him off, you know, but I was careful to see there's no record of it in the correspondence." He sat back and grinned as before.

Porter was nonplussed. "You mean we've been tryin' to get into what we thought was your territory—and it's really ours?"

"We don't have any witnesses here, so I'm going to say yes." Cobden laughed at his own admission, then sobered and leaned forward. "I'm selling the Lone Star for a pile to that old San Francisco moneybags on the basis that we're in bonanza at the eight-hundred-foot level. I'll admit I'm making a bundle on the deal! But a good businessman wants more—and I am a good businessman. What'll you pay me to deliver those letters from the surveyor?"

Porter growled something incomprehensible, and his face flushed with thought. "You really are a son-of-a-bitch, ain't you?" he rasped.

Cobden waved a confident hand. "Whatever else I might be, I *am* a good businessman!" he repeated. And he laughed in Porter's face. "You can't afford not to buy those letters," he said. "I know how close to the edge you are financially. And those letters can bring you the bonanza you need!"

There was a pregnant pause. Then Porter spoke up. "Five thousand," he said.

"Oh, don't make me laugh! If that's your level of thinking, I'm not going to waste any more of my time with you."

"I'll make it ten."

Cobden got out of his chair. "I don't think we're going to be able to do business—"

"Now, wait!" Porter pleaded. "I'm short o' cash. Otherwise I'd be willin' to pay fifty—and that's my top. But how'll I get it?"

Cobden nodded seriously. "I'd take fifty," he said. "And the way you get it is right in your lap."

"In my lap?"

"Yes. Finley's dead, isn't he? Doesn't that mean you own the whole damn thing? Borrow on it, for God's sake, borrow on it!"

Porter nodded with perception. "My partner's niece has a claim on it," he said, "but—"

"Well, you certainly ought to be able to handle that! Now, look!" Cobden shook a minatory finger under Porter's thick nose. "I want that deal completed before the breakthrough! I don't know what attitude Ward'll take when he finds out about the boundary line—and you haven't much time to find out. They're breaking through in a matter of hours! There's just one place I know of to go for that kind of ready money."

Porter rose as if in a trance from his chair. "Sharon?" he asked.

"You've named the one! And you'd better hurry. The deal's off if the breakthrough comes through first!"

Porter got to his feet. For a moment he was silent, looking down on the seated Cobden with a frown. Anyone could have told from his expression that his thoughts were not pleasant. "All right," he rasped. "I'll do what I can."

Cobden laughed. "You can do it," he reassured. "Not only that, you've *got* to!" And after Porter had left, he continued to smile, rubbing his hands together with satisfaction and returning to the account books before him.

CHAPTER 9

AL Porter had never met William Sharon, though it was impossible to live in Virginia City without knowing who he was. A small man, dapper and shrewd, with a drooping moustache, Sharon represented the Bank of California as well as William Chapman Ralston, its boss. The Bank of California had financed the Comstock. And Ralston had gambled on silver and won. He and his partners had made huge fortunes. He had built a fantastically luxurious palace some twenty miles south of San Francisco, and every morning he would race a superb team of carriage horses from his home in Belmont to his office in the city, clocking his departure and arrival with fanfare and precision. So important and colorful was he that if an important person were to visit San Francisco, he would be invited to Ralston's home in Belmont. And if he were not invited, his importance would be under a cloud.

But Ralston remained in the Bay Area to enjoy its many splendors, and was utterly dependent on Bill Sharon to defend his interests in Washoe.

Not that Sharon objected. He, too, had made a gigantic fortune and was as eager a gambler as his employer. On the sandy, treeless slopes of Sun Mountain Sharon lived like a king, drinking the finest of wines, eating the most costly viands, entertaining the prettiest women, and ruling the Comstock with a ruthless and iron hand.

No one could survive for long in Virginia City without a

determined will, and Al Porter himself was no soft touch. He had left New York in a hurry as the result of the authorities' nosing into his business dealings. In California he had been involved in swindling Mexican *rancheros* out of their landholdings. And, as the owner of the Nancy Belle, he had wound up with a mine with unproven prospects.

Despite his experience and hardened conscience, he was nervous as he entered the plush offices of the Virginia City branch of the Bank of California. Bill Sharon, he knew, loomed over the entire Comstock like some incubus, and his power derived from his importance in the bank. No man spoke of him without respect—and the more timid voiced his name with fear. The Bank of California having been the only large financial organization which had had the guts to risk its depositors' money in the gamble on silver—and having succeeded beyond Ralston's wildest dreams—it could make or break any businessman or miner in Washoe. And the man who decided when the bank's ax should fall was Bill Sharon.

Sharon's office was impressive. The outer building may have been board-and-batten with a graystone front, but even the anteroom to the office was paneled in polished oak, with deep green leather chairs dotted with many buttons. The young man with the high wing collar, pince-nez, and severe expression who guarded the door clearly was not pleased to see Porter in his shabby clothing.

"You have an appointment?" he inquired.

"No. I came to see Sharon, if he's in. If he's not, I'd like to make an appointment."

"*Mr.* Sharon seldom sees anyone without an appointment. What did you wish to see him about?"

"A loan."

"Well, I doubt—"

The door to the inner office swung open, and Sharon himself came out. He had clothed his small body in a beautifully fitted long greenish-gray coat, and under his instep-strapped pantaloons shone shiny boots of the most costly cordovan leather. His grizzled hair was brushed straight back, and a heavy moustache hid the unimpressive lower half of his face.

His eyes, however, were anything but unimpressive. They were sharp and cold and calculating, and they appraised Porter with quick efficiency. He removed a long Havana cigar from his mouth and addressed the secretary. "I was going out, but is this gentleman here to see me?"

"He wants a loan," the secretary sniffed.

Sharon replaced the cigar in his mouth and moved toward the outer door, pulling on a glove as he did so. "Tell him to put his request in writing—"

But Porter rose and stood in his way. "Mr. Sharon," he said, "I'm sole owner of the Nancy Belle, and we just struck a four-foot vein. I need some money—now."

Sharon halted, removed his glove, took the cigar from his mouth, smiled, and waved Porter toward the inner office. "A four-foot vein? Come in," he said. "I think we should talk."

Two hours later, Porter hurried to Cobden's office. Here he found things in an uproar. Cobden nodded wordlessly to him as he entered but continued to address the group of men around him and, from his words to them, Porter could tell that they had recently been hired. They were dressed in Levis and flannel shirts, and most of them carried weapons, either pistols or short-barreled shotguns. Eight in all, one was younger than the rest and looked surprisingly like Don Warren.

"They're about to break through!" Cobden announced. "You fellows must hold the ground and not let that gang from next door occupy any of our territory! And you"—he spoke to the young man at the head of the group—"try to avoid violence, but don't give up any of our claim. Now, go to it!"

The men, muttering and grinning—with the exception of the young man at their head, who was sober-faced—left the office and headed toward the shafthead with its elevator housing and steam donkey. Cobden took a deep breath and turned toward Porter.

"Did you get it? If you did, you're just in the nick o' time."

Porter nodded. "Fifty thousand." He pulled an envelope out of his pocket. "It's a bank draft. Sharon OK'd it himself."

Cobden seized the envelope, ripped it open, and examined the paper within. Then he pressed it to his lips—and when he took it away, they were spread in a grin. "Great!" he exclaimed exuberantly. "Now I can leave this hellhole and start livin' again! Here's what you paid for." He handed Porter another envelope.

"First call off your boys and stop the shootin' below."

Cobden laughed in his face. "Not on your life!" he bellowed. "If I did that, old man Ward in San Francisco might begin to wonder—and I don't want a thing to disturb him. He knows there's liable to be a row, and he'll expect me to take a strong position. Now, if you want to stop the row, you go right ahead and do it yourself!" He could hardly say it for laughing. "As for me, I'm goin' to San Francisco. Go ahead . . . enjoy your bonanza!"

Porter swore and left the office in haste.

CHAPTER 10

IN the steamy, breathless depths of the eight-hundred-foot level, Don Warren stopped to listen to the picks of the Lone Star on the other side of the rock wall that now was so thin that dust and pebbles fell from it as the miners on the other side thumped away at the vein.

Flaherty came to his side, mopping his dripping brow with a sweat rag. "It's gettin' wetter," he said. "Wouldn't surprise me none if there was another hot spring right in front of us."

A miner at the drifthead looked over his shoulder and cupped his hands to shout, "We're almost through! Watch yourselves!"

Flaherty jumped to attention and roared at the three hired guns who still were in the drift, making certain that digging progressed with all possible speed. "Over here!" he bellowed. "When we break through, *you* can go to work!"

The sounds of digging grew louder. The Nancy Belle's men were eager now to break a hole in the rock. They laughed and shouted and worked faster than before. The vein was widening. Now well over four feet, there was reason for haste—if Finley's recalculations could be believed.

Don Warren laid down his shovel and grasped a pick handle. Porter's men had brought down a few pistols, but he let them alone. He did not know what forces threatened on the other side of that rock barrier, but he did know about the sawed-off shotguns behind him, and he had seen the cold eyes of the men who held them. He even suspected that now that he had argued with Porter over Finley's niece's rights to the mine, Porter might want him to meet with an accident.

Suddenly he felt helpless—as if he were being dragged inexorably toward disaster. When he had informed Belden Ward that he wanted to see action, he had never in his wildest imaginings thought of anything like this. He took a deep breath of fetid air and straightened to ease his aching muscles. Sweat poured from his body. The heat was so great that even the pick handle felt hot. The oppressive humidity; the constant sound of trickling hot water; the thick darkness; the flickering torches; the heavy air, which never seemed to fill one's lungs—all made this cavern a genuine hellhole. And now, with the hired guns at his back, there was every possibility that he might be seriously wounded or killed in a stupid fracas which, with any application of common sense, could easily have been avoided.

The pounding of picks on the other side of the rock wall grew louder, and the Nancy Belle's miners redoubled their efforts, shouting encouragement to one another. Don Warren's stomach turned into a tight ball as the laboring, half-naked men, glistening with sweat under the moving, deep-shadowed torchlight, tore at the rock as if eager for battle.

Suddenly there was a shout from many throats. Rocks and pebbles crashed in a noisy shower to the floor of the drift. And through a black hole in the rock wall, Don Warren saw the shiny prong of a pick.

The Lone Star had broken through.

The hired guns ran forward, shouldering miners out of their way.

Greg Warren felt puzzled as he was swept along in the crowd of men hastening toward the elevator shed. He found himself jammed in a tight throng, crowded on the little platform, and he looked warily at the wire cable, wondering if it were strong enough to support this heavy weight of humans.

He had wanted some excitement—but this! His earlier brief

look at the eight-hundred-foot level under the guidance of Ben Steele, the underground foreman, had not been reassuring. The heat; the trickling water; the mud underfoot; the perspiring men, the thick, fetid air; and the gloom, only occasionally lightened by a combination of the yellow flickering lamps and the headlamps of the miners themselves—none of these had been in his calculations when he had welcomed Belden Ward's invitation to go to Virginia City to make certain that Ward's purchase of the Lone Star from Jim Cobden was an honest deal.

Greg caught his breath as the elevator operator apparently cut the power and let the platform drop with sickening speed into the dark depths of the mine. Rough rock walls of the shaft rushed past him, and Greg knew that if one stuck out an arm, or allowed himself to be pushed to the edge of the platform, whatever part of one's anatomy protruded would be ground to bloody pulp.

Suddenly the cable tightened, and with it the floor of the elevator seemed to push upward with terrific force, so that his knees bent and he was hard put to cling to the pipe crossbar, the only safety device afforded the elevator's passengers. Quickly the elevator came to a stop, bouncing slightly with the elasticity of the long cable. In the wall of the shaft a dark opening loomed, and the men clambered off the platform and into the black cave. Greg knew he was supposed to be leading this crew, but he found himself swept along in their midst with the uneasy feeling that most of those around him—bearded, profane, armed hard cases all—regarded him with amusement.

He could hardly arrange his thoughts. He had just arrived, for Pete's sake! Altogether he hadn't been in Virginia City more than a few hours, and already he was being carried into an odorous, stifling pit of hell, readying for a battle for which he had no stomach, to say nothing of little interest.

In an effort to recover some of his dignity, he hurried faster than the others and pushed himself to the head of the line. He hoped there were no branch drifts. His earlier trip with Ben

Steele had not been long enough to give him any assurance as to underground geography, and he realized that if two passages offered, he would not know which one to take. Fortunately, the Lone Star drift at the eight-hundred-foot level had no branches, and dim lamps every few yards assured him that they were indeed in the working mine.

As they hastened deeper into the mountain, he felt the oppressive weight of tons of earth and rock over his head and wondered if this cavern were to be his grave. The heat seemed to increase as they moved farther from the elevator shaft, and they splashed through pools made from trickling water on the rough floor. One of the pools was so hot he winced, and some of the men yelled with pain as the water splashed on bare arms and faces.

Then they were at the drifthead, with more lights on the rough walls, and around them the curious timber cribbing holding up the suddenly heightened roof of the cavern. Miners picking at the rock face and shoveling ore into the cars turned as he and the armed men arrived and burst into gleeful shouts, "We're almost through! Any minute now!"

Greg Warren found himself pushed by his followers to the very rock face, which seemed to be trembling from the pounding it was receiving from both sides. Suddenly he realized he was holding a gun in his hand. He remembered now. It had been thrust at him by Cobden as he urged his men to battle. It was a long-barreled, heavy-caliber five-shooter, and he looked at it with distaste. How did one fire the damn thing? You had to cock it first, he remembered.

There was a roar from the men. One of the miners had pierced the rock wall. A hole appeared, and the men continued to shout. There was noise coming through the hole as well, and as the hole rapidly enlarged he saw a flickering light on the other side. There were men there. He could see their picks coming through. And both sides were shouting with excitement, pounding and scrabbling away at the rock barrier.

The hole grew larger quickly. Bearded, grinning faces appeared through it. A miner from the Nancy Belle threw a booted leg over the lower rim of the hole, and one of the lone Star's men swung a mighty full-armed blow at it with a pick handle. The man howled with pain and withdrew a broken leg.

Greg grasped his gun tighter. This was hell—absolute hell.

On the Nancy Belle's side of the aperture, Don Warren dropped his pick handle and grasped the gun which had been dropped by the miner whose leg had been broken by the pick handle and who now was lying groaning on the ground and trying to crawl out of the way of the stamping, shouting, crowding men.

The hole widened suddenly as a large section of rock wall collapsed under the blows of the picks. There was a bright flash and a deafening roar from the other side as one of the armed men from the Lone Star fired through the hole. The miner next to Don cried out in pain and slumped to the ground. Don glanced down at him. He was bent over in agony, clutching his side, and blood was welling between his fingers. Don looked up again just in time to see the same gun muzzle that had fired before aimed squarely at his head. Don ducked and fired the gun in his hand reflexively. The man who had fired at him still kept climbing through the rocky aperture, so Don had missed, but a dark figure next to the man slumped down, halfway through. Don felt sick as he saw it. He had hit someone, but not the one he had aimed at.

The battle was joined. Men shouted, an occasional shot was fired, resounding with deafening thunder in the confines of the drift. Pick handles swung and sounded *thwuck!* on skulls. Men screamed in pain, and the stamping, thudding, sweating mob, swinging fists as well as weapons, merged into a howling, mad, free-for-all melee in the half-lit gloom. Don Warren gasped for air as he warded off blows and tried to fight his way toward the hole in the drifthead which was the center of the struggle. The man he had inadvertently shot still lay motionless, face down, half in the Lone Star, half in the Nancy Belle, his dark-clad body bent almost double by the rock barrier that still remained at the lower edge of the aperture.

Even as he fought, Don felt his stomach churn as he thought of the man he had probably killed. Damn Porter, who had forced this battle! This unnecessary, stupid, idiotic, painful, wounding combat was being fought over a vein of dirty ore!

Someone shouted. A roar arose which sounded different from the noise of battling men. Pounding feet suddenly drowned out other sounds.

"A spring!" a voice bellowed. "A boilin' spring! Run, damnit!"

With the quickness of a thunderclap, the battle ended. Water suddenly began to pour from a hole near the top of the drift wall—steaming, hot water. Men who had been struggling with one another and pushing toward the aperture in the rock wall now turned tail and scrambled as speedily as they could back along the drift toward the elevator shaft.

The same thing, apparently, was happening on the other side, in the Lone Star.

Don Warren turned with the others, threw down his gun, which already had unintentionally done more damage than he desired, and ran with them. As he did so, the roar of the rushing water increased. He glanced back. Huge sections of the drift wall above the vein were tumbling darkly onto the floor of the mine, thrust out by thousands of gallons of near-boiling water, which poured like a small Niagara from the subterranean reservoirs of the mountain.

Water already was around his ankles, and it was frighteningly hot. Steam was rising from the floor as the men splashed in panic away from that quickening flood. Again he looked back. The drift was empty—save for one pathetic figure. The dark-clad man he had mistakenly shot was still lying motionless across the lower rim of the rock barrier.

He halted. Men thrust past him, and one shouted in his ear, "Get goin'! You'll be scalded to death!"

The drift was becoming darker. Splashing water had extinguished two of the wall sconces.

The pathetic dark figure still lay there in the gloom.

The man might not be dead.

In a sudden resolve, Warren reversed his steps. Hastily he splashed back toward the drifthead. Water now was pouring with a deafening roar out of an opening—three or more feet in diameter near the roof of the drift—in a volume that threatened to fill the corridor and even the enlarged cribbed cavern that had been hollowed out to seek the widening vein. Water now was at his knees. And steam was rising around him, and he was breathing it. The water was painfully hot.

The man probably was dead.

Warren could lose his own life unless he fled with the others.

But now he was only a few feet from the slumped figure. Water was almost at the man's hanging head. If he were not already dead, he soon would be, drowned before he regained consciousness.

Stubbornly, Warren splashed toward him. Another boulder thumped out of the hot artesian spring and narrowly missed his head. It splashed behind him and was swept toward the elevator shaft by water which had risen well above his knees. A few more feet to go—but he could not stand much more. The water was rising and it was very hot.

He reached the unconscious man, grasped him under his arms, and lifted him to his shoulder. The man was totally limp, but he groaned as he was moved. He was still alive, then. The mission of mercy had not been in vain. Warren peered through the aperture toward the Lone Star drift to see if there were less water on that side , but it seemed worse. The flood was even deeper on the far side of the rock barrier, and the lights seemingly had all been quenched. It was utterly black beyond the hole in the rock.

Stubbornly, fear rising steadily within him, Don Warren struggled and splashed his way back toward the elevator. He and his pathetic burden were alone. The men were far ahead. Many frightening images came to his mind. Suppose the elevator itself were disabled by the flood? The water was deepening fast: It now was chest high. He knew the drift dipped down in midcourse before it reached the shaft. Suppose the water entirely filled it?

The rocky roof came closer, and the water, now shoulder high, almost reached it. He tried to move faster, but the hot water and the dank air—now small in quantity above the flood—made his panting labored. He was having trouble keeping his victim's head above the surface, and then—

A new surge of water thrust at his back, and the level rose almost to the drift's ceiling. He was swimming now, against the flood, his head bumping the roof of the drift. He knew that unless he could gain a footing, he and the man he was trying to save would drown.

The water filled the drift. He had to retreat, back toward the drifthead, back toward that enlarged chamber with the cribbing where he and his companion might find air above the churning waters.

He had to go back—away from rescue, away from the route to the upper world.

He fought and struggled on his backward path. Often his feet left the floor of the corridor, and he was swimming again. But then the drift rose toward the widening vein, and, dripping with water and his heart almost bursting, he—carrying his victim—half waded, half swam back toward the hollow frames of timbers which the German engineer Deidesheimer had invented to prevent cave-ins.

The water was still pouring out of the hole near the roof of the drift, but it was lessening in quantity, he noted with merciful relief. One sconce still burned near the vein. The others had been extinguished. His own cap lamp had been quenched long since. When that one sconce flickered out, there would be absolute blackness, a frightening dark that could not be pierced until his cap lamp dried out. Luckily he still had flint and steel—many miners had them for safety.

Gasping for air, he reached the timbered cribbing and

draped the sagging body of his companion across it. He had to wait a few moments to catch his breath, but when he did, he pulled himself up onto the timbering—and although the rough six-by-six was hardly comfortable, it was heavenly relief to get his body out of that uncomfortably warm, fetid pool.

After a time his panting slowed, and his thumping heart quieted. Only then did he feel he had the strength to turn to the limp figure next to him, precariously balanced on the timber.

He saw the wound he had himself inflicted. It was below the man's right shoulder, close to the chest cavity. He hoped it had not hit a lung. The heavy-caliber slug had produced shock enough to bring unconsciousness, but now the man was stirring and gasping for breath as he regained his senses.

Don Warren straddled the heavy beam and lifted the man's head to permit him to breathe more easily. As he did so, he gave a start that came near to upsetting both him and the other into the water. Again Don's heart thudded against his ribs, and a cold sense of shock rose within him.

He gazed again upon the other's face. He could not believe his eyes. He was not mistaken.

It was the face of his younger brother, Greg.

Don's pulse pounded. He must be dreaming. His hands shook as he held the other's shoulders.

At that moment the water level reached the wall lamp on the drift's side, and the light flickered out.

He and his brother were in utter, absolute, frightening blackness that smothered them like a heavy blanket.

Greg stirred and groaned in his arms. And as he felt the movement and heard the pitiful sound, Don Warren clenched his jaw and held as tightly to his emotions as he did to the rough cribbing which kept them from the inky, steaming depths below.

CHAPTER 11

IN the town, under the hot Nevada sun, word of the war in the drifts had spread, and the populace, accustomed to violence and excitement, was attracted as by a magnet to the area surrounding the shacky outbuildings of the two warring mines.

On the Lone Star side, reporters ranted boisterously and gesticulated wildly, trying to learn the whereabouts of Jim Cobden.

"Where is he?" one demanded. "Why in hell would he be away at a time like this?"

"He prob'ly didn't know the breakthrough was this close," one volunteered.

"Well, he should have. They've been close for days. He *must've* known it was about to happen!"

The male secretary, wringing his hands and almost in tears, kept protesting that he had no idea where Mr. Cobden had gone, that Ben Steele would be the one to talk to, but he was down in the mine.

At the Nancy Belle, Al Porter chewed his cigar from one corner of his mouth to the other and waited by the elevator, grinning. Men clustered around him, questioning, probing.

"It's all right," he said, waving his cigar at them. "It ain't that serious."

"Whaddaya mean, it ain't serious?" a whiskered oldster who clearly had spent years in the mines demanded. "A drift war, and you ain't even excited! What the hell!"

"Naw, I got plenty of men down there."

"That ain't it!" the old man yelled in Porter's ear. "They's fellers gittin' killed and hurt! It's hell down there!"

"How do we know that?" Porter asked, trying to calm him and others who hung at his heels. "All I know is, I got word from below that they broke through."

"We know what's been goin' on around here!" the old man screamed. "We know what's been goin' on at the Lone Star! They's enough guns down there on both sides to field a army! We don't have to see it to know there's blood runnin' in those drifts!"

In town, the screeching steam whistles—with their short, sharp, frightening blasts heralding an emergency—penetrated the walls of Sarah Finley's boardinghouse room just off C Street. She listened for a time; then, fearing the worst, nervously made her way to the center of town and on past it toward the slopes of Sun Mountain. By this time men and women were thronging the streets, heading in the same direction.

"What is it?" she asked anxiously, but several pushed by her without responding. Finally, a hustling miner took pity on her and called back over his shoulder, "War in the drifts, sister! It's the Nancy Belle!"

Cold panic clutched her, and as soon as she got ahold of herself, the words made her want to hurry as fast as the others. She lifted her skirts and began to run, desperately and breathlessly, toward the slopes. At the entrance to the side street where Emma Nelson's cafe was located, Sarah came upon Emma herself, lumbering ponderously along the boardwalk, panting and puffing her way toward the mines.

"Emma!" she cried. "It's the Nancy Belle! They've broken through! And Don's down there!"

The big woman nodded wordlessly, grabbed the girl's hand, and together they made their way up the steep, dusty slope, now crowded with sightseers.

As they arrived at the Nancy Belle elevator shack, an

elevatorful of haggard, perspiring, earth-streaked miners reached the surface and tumbled out onto the platform. Frantic, Sarah pushed past Emma Nelson and elbowed her way through the crowd until she could see the faces of the men.

"He's not there!" she cried.

Emma placed a large hand over hers and patted it.

"There'll be other loads, dearie," she said. "But why are they comin' up?"

"Flood! Boilin' spring! Git that elevator down here afore the shaft's flooded too!"

The words were flung out first by one and then another, and were repeated again and again, louder and louder.

Sarah's heart sank. She gripped Emma's arm for support.

"A flood!" Sarah exclaimed, her eyes bright. "And boiling water! Don told me men have been scalded to death—and drowned. What'll we do? He's not up yet!"

Even as she spoke, the elevator rumbled downward. But as the cries of the flooded drift spread, Al Porter, who had managed to extricate himself from the crowd and had reentered his office, came out again, this time with a worried look on his face.

Sarah ran toward him. "Is Don all right?" she asked. "Is he still below?"

"He's all right," Porter blustered. "We had enough men down there to take care of anything."

But his eyes told her another story.

"Of course," he added, "if they've hit another one o' those damn springs—" He pulled away and hurried to the elevator, where he conversed with the operator.

Another elevator load of men popped to the surface, and again Sarah examined every perspiring, dirt-streaked face. She clutched Emma's arm tighter. "He's not there!" Sarah wailed.

"There must be another load!" Emma said grimly. "Now, don't you worry. He's goin' to be all right."

A third load came, and once again Sarah searched every face. Pat Flaherty, the huge Irishman, was the last one off. He was naked to the waist, his barrel chest covered with a shag of reddish hair. Sweat poured from him.

Sarah made a dash for him. "Mr. Flaherty! There's another load, isn't there? Isn't there still another?"

He regarded her sorrowfully and shook his head. "No, *mavourneen*. An' there won't be any more men comin' up the way they went down. Abe Stilson ain't ever comin' up. He was shot by one of those bastards from the Lone Star. An' the other—"

"The other—" Sarah paled and felt faint. "Tell me, Pat. Who was the other?"

"That other casualty wasn't the Warren boy, was it?" Emma put in.

Flaherty nodded. "It was hell down there," he began. "When the boys busted through into that hot spring, as they was openin' up the hole in the breakthrough to the Lone Star, Warren was behind us, but runnin'. But he'd shot a feller from Lone Star, an' I seen him stop and go back to save him. I yelled to him to forgit the other an' hurry with us, but the water was steamin' an' churnin' around our ankles, and a-rushin' through that hole in the wall like a waterfall. Don still was splashin' in the wrong direction—toward that feller he'd shot, last time I saw him. I knew we had to hurry. That drift had a drop of eight feet in it before it got to the elevator shaft, and at the rate that water was comin' in, I knew it would fill the tunnel. Then nobody would git through. It was gettin' too hot." He laid a hand on the girl's arm. "I'd a'tried to save him—but if a man feels he's got to do somethin' and thinks it's more important then bein' saved, why—"

Sarah froze as she listened.

And Emma Nelson felt instinctively that it was time to put her large arm around her.

"You mean—" Sarah finally faltered, "you mean—"

"Warren's dead," Flaherty said flatly. "It hurts me to say it, foine boy that he was. But there ain't no way a human bein' could have got out of that steamy, splashin' mess!"

Her arms still around the shoulders of the weeping girl, Emma Nelson led her slowly away from the mine.

Al Porter had other ideas and hastened forward to block their way.

"Am I to understand that Warren gave you your uncle's copy of our partnership agreement?" he asked belligerently. "Well, I'm the surviving partner, and now the whole thing belongs to me. I'd appreciate your giving me that copy of the agreement."

Sarah perked up and wiped her eyes. "There's no mention of survivorship in it," she said. "Don told me so. So you won't be needing that paper. I've inherited my uncle's share."

"That's the ticket, dearie," Emma Nelson encouraged. "Stand on yer rights! B'sides," she glared at Porter, "ain't there somethin' in the law that says that if you shoot yer partner, you run into trouble if you try to take over yer dead partner's share?"

The crowd was milling noisily, and the mine whistles still were screeching their tocsin of disaster. Porter stepped closer, his plump face dark with anger.

"I want that agreement!" he insisted. "And I want it now! I'm givin' you 'til this afternoon to git it to me. If I don't have it by then, I'm comin' after it. Don't play games with me, lady!" he warned.

Emma Nelson thrust her massive bulk between them. "This poor girl ain't in any mood to argy with you, Al Porter! Not after you shot her uncle—and with her boyfriend down in that hellhole. You jist stay away from her!"

"I want that agreement!" he repeated stubbornly. "And before the day's out. I'm warnin' you. If you don't bring it to me, I'll come and git it!"

The two women pushed past him and descended the dusty hill. "Don't give in to him!" Emma advised the girl. "You hang onto that paper. What you need is a lawyer!"

"But what if he comes over to get it?" Sarah's voice shook just thinking about it. I'm all alone—"

Emma clamped her lips decisively. "You go git that paper and come back an' stay with me for a while. Al Porter won't do nothin' to you if you're stayin' with me!"

A man in a checked suit with tight-fitting trousers, topped with a derby, halted before them. Removing the derby, he managed a courtly bow. He was looking at Sarah Finley.

"I noted your despair, ladies. May I be of help? I take it somebody you know is still down in the mine."

"Who're you?" Emma demanded.

"Ed Musgrove at your service, ma'am. I've just arrived in town, and I've come to see what all the excitement is about." He glanced again, appreciatively, at Sarah. "I mean it, ladies. If there is any way I can be of help in this sad moment, I offer my services."

Emma Nelson's eyes narrowed as she gazed piercingly at the man's face. "If you mean what you say," she said, "you can come with us and help us git a piece o' paper that somebody nasty is tryin' to take away from this poor girl. I think three o' us would be more'n a match fer Al Porter."

Mr. Musgrove, on closer view, became wholly fascinated with Sarah's appearance. "Anything!" he agreed expansively. "If I can be of the least bit of help, please call on me."

"We're callin' now!" Emma announced decisively. "Come along. An' if you got a gun, it might help."

"A gun!"

For a moment Mr. Musgrove appeared hesitant. Then another glance at Sarah Finley's perfect features decided him, and he straightened and firmed his jaw. "I have no gun," he said, "but I do have this walking stick! I shall be glad to serve as your protector!"

"Good!" Emma grunted. "Keep yer eye peeled fer a fat tub o' lard with a mean expression—the feller we was just talkin' to. He's the one who'll be after us."

Mr. Musgrove raised his stick like a baton. "Onward!" he said. "You lead the way!"

CHAPTER 12

AT the eight-hundred-foot level, balanced uncomfortably on the rough timbers of the cribbing, Don Warren sat in absolute blackness, trying to explain to his brother what had happened.

Greg was in pain and groaned with every move—but he had regained consciousness and was attempting to understand Don's words.

"I had no idea you were working for the Nancy Belle," Greg said, his voice strained and weak from the shock of his wound. "And I don't think Mr. Ward did either."

"He knew where I was working, all right, but he didn't know the Nancy Belle and the Lone Star were next to each other. How are you feeling, kid?"

"Not good," Greg said after a pause. "I think I've stopped bleeding, but it hurts like the devil."

"Well, we've got to get you out of here so a doctor can look at your shoulder. The water's going down, and as soon as I can, I'll try to light that wall lamp so we can see."

"Even if you can, what good'll that do if the drift's flooded?"

"I told you the water's going down."

Don Warren spoke decisively—as much to bolster his own feelings as to reassure his brother. "As long as there's air space above it, we'll get out!"

They waited and listened as the water gurgled and the out-pouring from the spring above their heads diminished to a trickle. After what seemed hours, Don thought he could make a stab at it. "I'm going to try to light that lamp on the wall,"

117

he told Greg, "if I can find it. Can you balance yourself while I'm gone?"

"Go ahead," Greg said weakly. "I'll be all right."

The thinness of his voice troubled Don, but it added to his haste. Unless they had light, they could not see to escape; and unless they escaped, they would be in the bowels of the earth forever.

"Lean your head against this upright," Don urged, "and straddle the beam. If you feel faint, grab the upright and holler. I'll come right away."

"Hurry back," Greg whispered.

Don lowered himself from the beam into the hot water. The water had gone down—far enough so that it came only to his waist. He was encouraged. At that rate, the flooded drift between them and the elevator shaft might even be passable. Carefully he waded toward the rock wall, groped for the lamp, and—at first—could not find it. A knot of panic rose in his stomach until he did. "Found it!" he called back. But his brother did not answer. Dear God, had Greg lost consciousness? Don had heard no splash. Apparently Greg still was straddling the beam.

It was *so* dark—a frightening blackness without a pinpoint of relief. It was oppressive, overpowering. This must be how a blind person felt. How terrible to be blind! One could see nothing—absolutely nothing. The blackness lay all about, and it was all Don could do to keep the unreasonable squirmings of panic from rising in his throat.

Waist deep in uncomfortably warm water, the exposed parts of his body dripping with sweat, he got out his flint and steel and tried to make it work. But everything was so wet that for a time the sparks were extinguished immediately. He pinched the wick of the lamp, trying to dry it off so the oil would start sucking. He tried again. And again he failed. From across the chamber he heard Greg groan. It *had* to work! They *had* to have light. He flicked the spark again. And again it went out. Maybe if he held the flint closer to the wick? He struck it again. And again.

Was it never going to work? Were they doomed to die in this black grave with tons of rock above their heads? In desperation, he gave it all he had. This time it flared.

The wick caught. Blessed, blessed light! Just that little flame on the wall—flickering over the water's surface and above, on the dripping walls—buoyed his spirits so unbelievably that he permitted himself a long, trembling sigh. With it, the knot of panic in his stomach subsided.

One victory!

Now for the other: escape!

Slowly and with tremendous effort, he made his way back through the waist-deep water to his brother's side. Greg now was moaning softly with every breath. Don was deeply worried. They would have to wade and swim out of this cavern, and that took effort. Was Greg capable of it? If not, Don would not leave him to die alone in this black hole.

"Greg," he said, "I've got the wall lamp lit, and from it, my cap lamp, and now we've got to try to get out of here. Are you up to it?"

"I think so," said Greg weakly. "But we'd better hurry. I'm feeling worse by the minute."

"Not bleeding again, is it?"

"Not that I can tell. But my head's spinning."

Carefully Don lifted Greg off the timber, eliciting a grunt of pain from him. "Hang on to my shoulders," Don said. "And if you want to rest, say so. We'll take it slow."

Feeling for every step, they waded through the deep, warm water. One stumble into a hole, and they might have to return to relight the cap lamp from the wall sconce.

One step at a time, side by side, they made their way toward the black hole in the wall. It was a major goal—the entrance to the drift that led to the Nancy Belle elevator shaft, and after they got there, Greg moaned. "Got to get my strength back," he said, panting.

Don waited a while, then cast a final look at the shadowy big chamber with its wooden cribbing and led the way into the black, water-filled tunnel. "We're going to be all right," he concluded, speaking bravely to his brother over his shoulder. "Even when the drift dips, it's not going to be above our heads." He prayed his conclusion was correct—but he was not at all certain.

The truth was otherwise.

The drift floor declined, and as it did, the water rushed to their waists, then crept to their chests. And still the floor sloped downward.

This had to be the drop that Flaherty had talked about. Don had not noticed that it was so sharp and evident when the drift was dry. Now, flooded, every inch of slope became a matter of concern.

Greg's arms slipped from his shoulder and, panicky, Don turned swiftly to catch him.

"Sorry," Greg said, gasping. "Arms slipped, that's all."

But Don knew his brother was losing what little strength he had. The shock of the bullet was not wearing off.

Foot by foot they proceeded, the water rising as high as their chins, then—to Don's tremendous relief—going down to their shoulders.

"We're past the deep part!" he assured.

But the words were hardly out of his mouth before the floor dropped sharply. Don knew their next steps would bring them into deep water.

The lamp flickered on the damp roof of the tunnel, which, five feet ahead of them, descended below the water's surface.

"We'll just wait here a few minutes until the water goes down a little more," Don said, trying to keep the tremor out of his voice.

"Something's wrong, isn't it?" Greg asked faintly.

"Water's still too deep in this low spot," Don answered, still trying to sound unworried. "But you can see it's lowering."

It was, but slowly—*very slowly*. How much farther would it have to subside before they could get through—if they ever did?

The knot of panic rose anew in Don's stomach, and his throat constricted.

CHAPTER 13

EMMA Nelson and Sarah Finley, accompanied by Mr. Musgrove, the traveling salesman in sewing kits, hastened down C Street in the direction of the boardinghouse where Sarah lived and in which the partnership agreement between her deceased uncle and Al Porter lay.

It lay in quite an obvious place—atop her dresser, and Sarah knew that if Porter reached there before them, he would not have the slightest trouble finding it.

"What a shame," Emma panted as they hurried along, "that of all the men in the mine, that fine boy had to be stuck down below!"

"And it happened to him while he was saving someone!" Sarah grieved. "He gave his life for someone else!"

Exhausted by the effort of their fast walk, Emma did not remind her that Flaherty had said that Don Warren indeed had been saving a man, but a man he had shot.

They turned off C Street and descended silently down the gulley and up the far slope to the boardinghouse, and at its door Mr. Musgrove hastened to open it for them, then bowed them in with courteous aplomb. Sarah then took the lead and bolted up the stairs ahead of them, opening the door leading into her own room. There, prominently placed on the dresser, she saw the important partnership agreement she was after.

"You hadn't oughter leave anything as important as this layin' around," Emma admonished, shaking her head.

"Oh, I know," Sarah concurred. "I don't know why I did. I forgot all about it and ran when I heard the mine whistles."

"Anyways, we got here first," Emma said, closing the subject as she watched Sarah fold the paper and place it in her large purse.

Mr. Musgrove bowed again. "This is what you came for, ladies?" he inquired. "You have it now. May we depart?"

Emma faced him squarely. "You got to stay with us—with that stick—until we git back to my restaurant! This little girl is goin' to stay with me for a while. But we got to git back there first!"

Mr. Musgrove bowed a third time, his eyes fixed on Sarah Finley's perfect profile. "Ladies, I am at your service!"

The three left Sarah's apartment, which she locked tightly. From there they proceeded down the dusty street, up the slope to C Street, and were proceeding down toward Emma Nelson's cafe, when—

"All right! I'll just take it now—to save you the trouble of bringing it to the Nancy Belle!"

Al Porter stood before them, feet spread apart, chunky body stubbornly blocking the way.

Emma Nelson moved toward him, her huge form resembling a battleship on the attack.

Porter did not flinch.

"You're not takin' anythin' from this girl!" Emma declared decisively. "It was her uncle who owned half o' that mine—and she's entitled to a copy o' that agreement!"

Porter protruded his stubbly jaw. "Her uncle's dead! His share belongs to *me*!"

"We're goin' to let some lawyers figure that out!" Emma blazed.

Sarah Finley spoke for the first time. "Mr. Porter, you must be enough of a gentleman to permit me to get some legal advice before I turn over all of my uncle's claims to you."

Porter moved forward, his face ugly. "Give me that

agreement!" he demanded. "We'll talk after I have it—but not until I have it!"

Emma turned to Mr. Musgrove. "Where the hell are you and your stick?"

Mr. Musgrove had been watching and listening. Every inner voice told him to get the hell out of there and save his skin, but he repeatedly glanced at Sarah Finley's profile, and every glance caused serious hesitation.

He moved forward. "Sir," he said, addressing Porter, "is it not possible for you to let this lady have her copy of the agreement—whatever it is—and discuss the matter peacefully at a later time? This is no way to conduct business—on the street!"

"It is to me!" said Porter. He stretched out his hand. "Give me that agreement!"

Mr. Musgrove cleared his throat decisively. He stood somewhat hesitantly between the women and Al Porter. The latter hunched his head between his shoulders and clenched his fists.

"Get out of my way!" Porter commanded.

But Musgrove only swallowed uncomfortably and shifted his feet.

Porter took a step forward. Musgrove raised his stick. Porter seized it, wrenched it free from Musgrove's grasp. Then he turned with the stick upon the salesman and rained a shower of hard blows upon his head and shoulders. Sarah and Emma saw the derby crushed, saw Musgrove, despite his good intentions, cower under the blows and raise his arms to shield himself from the attack.

"My God!" Emma breathed.

Sarah stood horrified and aghast.

The drummer was not of the stuff of heroes and was by no means a fighter. He withstood the asault for a long moment, then with a muttered, "Sorry, ladies!" he pulled his ruined hat down over his ears and beat a hasty retreat. Porter followed him for a few steps, then turned back as Musgrove continued to run until he was a block distant. Then he turned and looked back, but he made no attempt to retrace his steps.

As for Al Porter, he stood panting, Musgrove's stick gripped in his thick hand. Menacingly he approached the two. Emma Nelson looked around for help, but the street was strangely empty in their immediate vicinity. There were pedestrians, but they were many yards away and assiduously looking in other directions.

"Give me that agreement!" Porter grated. He thrust out a heavy hand.

For a long moment Sarah Finley hesitated, then she gave in and handed him the paper. Porter snatched it, tossed the stick to the ground, whirled on his heel, and departed in the direction of Musgrove's retreat. The salesman saw him coming and quickly disappeared around a corner.

Sarah and Emma gazed forlornly at each other.

Emma swore. "If only that Warren boy had been here, 'stead o' that white-livered, check-suited poor excuse, we'd a'held onto it!"

"Mr. Musgrove tried," said Sarah hopelessly.

Emma put her arm around the girl's shoulders. "We'll figger out somethin'!"

Sarah said nothing, but her eyes revealed that she did not agree even with Emma's restrained optimism.

In San Francisco, Belden Ward sat in his office on Montgomery Street and opened a letter which had just arrived by stage.

Belden Ward, Esq.

Dear Sir:
    I am happy to report that all papers are in order, and that you are now the new owner of the Lone Star Mine. This is to acknowledge receipt of the certified check drawn on the Bank of California, completing the sale.

I shall be leaving for the East shortly. I commend you to my foreman, Ben Steele, who is now *your* foreman. At least, I hope you'll keep him. He's a good man.

One piece of bad news. As you know, we've been arguing with the mine next door over claim lines, and fighting has broken out over the issue. Mr. Porter, the owner of the Nancy Belle (the mine which is our unfriendly neighbor) is difficult to deal with.

All of my stock shares in the Lone Star have been turned over to the Washoe branch of the Bank of California.

I wish you luck.

> Yr. obt. servant,
> /s/ James Cobden

Belden Ward was on his feet, clutching the paper, staring at it, breathing stertorously.

"The Nancy Belle!" he exclaimed. "My God! That's where Don is!"

He ran to the door and yelled for his secretary. The man responded hurriedly, polishing his glasses with nervous fingers.

"I'm going to Washoe!" Ward snapped. "Right away!" Get me tickets on the first Morgan Stage. I'm going home to pack. Back in a jiffy."

The secretary watched as Ward headed for the office door. Just short of it, Ward turned, his eyes narrowed. "Get me all the information you can on Jim Cobden," he ordered. I should have insisted on a lot more detail! The more I think about it, the less I like the way he's handled this deal. Hop to it!"

The flustered secretary wrung his hands and nodded energetically. But Belden Ward didn't see him as he left, slamming the office door.

Later, as Concord rattled and rumbled along the hot and

dusty road to Sacramento, Ward sat tensely and scowled at the landscape, seated in the rear between two red-shirted miners. From his pocket he pulled out the agreement he had made with Cobden and scanned it carefully.

The important thing Cobden's letter had told him was that the claim dispute had erupted into violence. And he, Ward, had sent Don's brother, Greg, to work for the Lone Star!

If there was violence, and if the two were involved, it was brother against brother. Ward folded the paper and groaned.

The stage gained speed as it rolled down the slopes of the coastal range into the vast yellow flatness of the Sacramento Valley.

CHAPTER 14

AT the eight-hundred level in the Nancy Belle, chin deep in hot water, supporting his brother on his back and hoping and praying that the candle in his miner's cap would not burn out, Don Warren watched the water level in the drift slowly recede. He wondered if he should go back to the cavern at the end of the drift to take refuge again on the framework of cribbing. At least they could dry off. But the prospect of a second retreat was so discouraging that he decided against it.

The water *was* going down, wasn't it?

He took comfort from the fact that a jutting rock in the drift wall, which had been nearly covered a short time ago, now was exposed a few more inches in the dim light of his cap candle. But it was maddeningly slow.

Greg, limp on his shoulders, half supported by the water, stirred painfully and groaned.

"Are you holding out all right?" Don asked. "It'll be only a little while until we can make a try at getting to the other side of this dip in the drift."

He hoped his optimism was not falsely based. Yet he knew it was. How in the world could he—with his wounded, almost helpless brother on his back—swim even for a few feet underwater—and hot, acrid water at that—to gain the other side of that dip in the rock roof? And how long was the dip? Suppose they swam several feet, found they could not continue, and could not make it back? Don shivered despite the heat of the water in which he was immersed. This would be their grave.

And such a terrible way to die, alone in the darkness with the mountain overhead.

He looked again at the protruding rock in the wall. The water was down another inch. But still it lapped against the roof of the drift ahead. How soon should they try to make it? He must not let panic drive him to make an attempt too early. How long would it be?

"I'm all right," Greg said weakly, anticipating his brother's question. "But can we try to make it pretty soon?"

At that moment the candle in Don's cap went out, and it told him what their next step must be. They had to return to the cavern at the head of the drift, where the wall sconces still flickered yellowly.

Discouraged, weak with fatigue and strain, fear he found hard to swallow bubbling up from within, he turned and sloshed back toward the drifthead.

"What—what are we doing?" Greg asked hoarsely, fear in his voice.

"Greg, boy," said Don with forced heartiness, "we've got to go back to relight my cap light. But by the time we're back, the water'll be low enough for us to get out of this place."

There was a gloomy silence as, with effort, they retreated through the gurgling water.

"I hope you're right," Greg whispered in Don's ear. "Oh, I do hope you're right."

CHAPTER 15

HERR Adolf Sutro, side whiskers neatly groomed, derby and brown knee-length coat immaculate, marched up the steps of the Nancy Belle's office and knocked on the door. He waited a moment, then knocked again.

Finally the door opened and the angry red face of a rotund man, cigar in a corner of his mouth, peered out.

"Who is it?" he demanded. "What do you want?"

Sutro lifted his hat and bowed slightly. "Is it that I address *Herr* Porter, owner of this mine?"

"Yeah, I'm Porter."

"Well, my name is Sutro. And I should like to talk with you, if I may."

Porter's brows shot up. "Sutro? Adolf Sutro? The feller who's building the tunnel?"

"I haf that honor."

"Well, I don't know what business we could have with each other," Porter said grudgingly. "But come on in. Remember now, I ain't got much time."

Sutro entered, seated himself on the edge of a chair, and removed his hat.

"Well?" Porter said. "I ain't got all day."

"I understand your mine iss flooded and that there are men still down there."

"Well, they're dead by now," Porter barked. "Everybody who could make it came up."

"That iss not necessarily so." Sutro was calm but insistent.

"I haf been talking with your foreman, Flaherty. He said your assistant, Mr. Warren, hurried back to the drifthead to save another man who was hurt, but by the time he returned, water had filled a low point in the drift. But there iss plenty of air in the drifthead. It iss a large cavern, I understand."

Porter shook his head impatiently. "What could I do about it even if they are still alive?"

"You can give me permission to drive a stope up to your eight-hundred-foot level and drain out the mine. I haf examined the surveys. In twenty-four hours I can do this."

"And then you'll ask for two dollars off the top of every ton of ore I dig," Porter snapped. "Nothing doing! I ain't going to be milked out of my profits!"

"But it costs money to extend my tunnel!" Sutro argued. "I am not a wealthy man, and the price iss not unreasonable!"

Porter rose, his chunky body hunched and belligerent. "I got no more time to talk. I told you I was busy—"

"But human lives are at stake!" Sutro made no move to rise from his chair.

"That's what you say! But there's nobody alive in that mine, the way I see it—and you're not goin' to use that argument to get me to sign away my profits! Now, get out! I'm through talkin'! Get out of my office!"

Sutro was horrified. He got to his feet, slowly. "You would not spend a few dollars to save lifes? Even when my tunnel will make your mine more profitable? It will enable you to dig deeper—"

"Yeah—at two dollars a ton!" Porter laughed scornfully. Now, get out! I've got work to do!"

Shaking his head, Adolf Sutro left the office. Outside it he halted, placed his derby on his head, looked back at the door of the Nancy Belle, glanced at the elevator shack, shook his head again dispiritedly, and walked down the hill.

At its base he almost collided with a young woman who was hurrying in the opposite direction.

"I beg your pardon, Miss—"

He lifted his hat to her.

"Oh, I'm sorry!" she apologized. "I guess I'm in too big a hurry." Her eyes widened. "Aren't you Mr. Sutro?" she asked excitedly. "I heard you give a talk about your tunnel the other evening."

He bowed gallantly. "That I am. It iss a pleasure to meet you, Miss—"

"Finley," she prompted hurriedly. "Mr. Sutro, can you please help? The Nancy Belle's flooded and—and there are men down there! Could your tunnel—?"

His head began to shake from side to side, and he sighed. "I haf just offered my services to the owner of the Nancy Belle."

"To Mr. Porter?" She was eager.

"He wass not interested."

"Not interested!" Sarah Finley paled. "I was hurrying to see him to beg him to do something—anything!" Tears began to well in her eyes.

Sutro regarded her sympathetically. "The man still in the mine—he iss a friend?"

She nodded. She was almost sobbing. "Yes. He is a friend. And I am so afraid he is—dead!"

Sutro shook his head. "It iss not necessary that he iss dead. There iss air in the chamber. More than enough for two men for many hours. Also, they haf broken through into the Lone Star. Air will be coming down that shaft. It iss not at all necessary that they are dead. But the water must be drained out or they will not escape."

She clutched his arm. "You know about mines. Do you really mean that? Is there a chance he is still alive?"

Sutro nodded solemnly. "I do not lie. What iss needed iss to drain the *Wasser. Und* I can do that. But Mr. Porter, he will not let me."

The girl was frantic. "He won't *let* you! Then he's condemning him to death! If you know there's a chance he's still alive, you *must* try. You cannot let a man die because Mr. Porter is—stubborn! And selfish!" She seized his arm again, desperation in her voice, tragedy in her eyes. "Please! If you can do something, please, please—I beg you—please do it!"

Adolf Sutro regarded her with kindly, thoughtful eyes. She was a beautiful girl, he thought, much like his little cousin in Hanover—the beautiful, smooth white skin; the dark hair; the large, lustrous eyes now filled with fear and pleading. Yes, she was much like his cousin. And if his cousin were begging for help from a stranger, he would wish that stranger to respond. He looked long at her tearful, desperate face, the agony in her gaze—

"I am not a wealthy man, *Liebchen*," he said. "And it costs money, much money, to dig in Sun Mountain—"

"I have a little," she said. "I will gladly give it to you. If you can do something, please, *please* do it!"

"No, no," he answered. "I am not asking you for anything. I am talking to myself. I think I have about won the argument."

"What do you mean?"

"I will run a stope to the eight-hundred-foot level of the Nancy Belle. And I will do it tonight. I probably will be sued by Mr. Porter. But if I can save the life of your friend, I will do so."

She kissed him.

Mr. Sutro was embarrassed. But despite the embarrassment, he thoroughly enjoyed the kiss and considered it more than sufficient recompense for the risks and expense he was assuming in draining the water in the Nancy Belle.

CHAPTER 16

AL Porter's thoughts were not pleasant. He had tried not to think about what was happening at the eight-hundred-foot level, and although he was not a sensitive man, he had sufficient imagination to contemplate what his own involvement might be if he failed to take every possible step to save a miner's life. There would be lawsuits, charges, court appearances, and, damnit, the man stuck down below was a former employee of Belden Ward. On top of that, he was extremely friendly with Sarah Finley, the niece of his late partner, about whom questions still might be asked.

He opened a drawer in his desk and removed the survey reports which Jim Cobden had given him for fifty thousand dollars.

He thumbed through them. They did everything Cobden had said they would. The surveys and the correspondence proved beyond a doubt that the Nancy Belle's claim extended well into what had been commonly assumed to be the Lone Star's territory.

He rubbed his chin. Maybe it would be sensible for him to take these documents to Sharon, borrow more money, and decamp. Things were getting pretty complicated. Then again, if he crossed Sharon and disappeared with some of Sharon's dollars, he was certain his future was limited.

Al Porter chewed the cigar from one side of his mouth to the other and thought. He was not used to thinking, and it bothered him, but he scowled and cudgeled his brain.

Wherever he turned, there were complications. One thing

was clear: He was not going to pay Adolf Sutro two dollars a ton! Now that the Nancy Belle was in bonanza he was not going to mortgage its future profits, even if it meant the death of Don Warren and the death of whomever Warren had been trying to save when he quixotically retreated as the last group of men rushed to the shaft.

Ed Musgrove, the traveler in sewing kits, slumped over a table in the Oriental and nursed his whiskey.

He was not feeling up to par. Customarily of an ebullient, cheerful disposition, he found the bases of his personality shattered and without foundation. It was bad enough to have been browbeaten and whipped by Al Porter on a public street, but worse to have had it happen before two ladies whom he had promised, Galahad-like, to protect and defend. He wondered if he ever would survive the memory of that awful morning.

He took another drink, ordered a second, downed that, and decided, on the basis of his Dutch courage, that he had to do something to recover his self-respect. But what? Making a few more sales would not suffice. His eyes ranged over the gathering at the long bar: red-shirted miners; tallow-spotted miners; coughing, gaunt miners; a sprinkling of nattily dressed individuals who were either businessmen or promoters; and the bar girls with their spangled short skirts, dark stockings, bare arms, and décolletages.

The bar girls! There, among them, was the pretty, hard-faced blond who had ridden with him over the Sierra from Sacramento. She had rejected him summarily in favor of that young Warren fellow who was signed up with one of the mines, and the way she had treated him had hurt his pride. What could be more salutary for his self-esteem than to score a point or two with Miss Birdie Boynton? As an employee of the Oriental, she could hardly scorn him now.

Mr. Musgrove sauntered over to the bar where Miss Boynton was standing. He doffed the hat and bowed low. "Miss Boynton, I believe," he began. "You remember me, the passenger on the stage from Sacramento? It's a pleasure to see you again."

She performed as expected. Her chin rose high and she regarded him arrogantly from half-closed lids. "Well, it's no pleasure to see you again," she sniffed. "You not only accosted me without an intraduction on that trip—me, a poor, defenseless, unescorted girl—but now you've made yourself the talk o' the town by gettin' beat up in public by Al Porter." She archly adjusted her back hair. "Mr. Porter's done me the favor of makin' my acquaintance, and he's a real *man*! He told me you cringed and ran like a whipped puppy."

Mr. Musgrove fingered his hat. "But did Porter tell you *why* he beat me up?"

"Sure. You were insolent to him, an' he taught you a lesson."

"He's a liar," said Mr. Musgrove, feeling his whiskey. "I was polite as hell. What he was doin' was stealin' a partnership agreement from that girl I was with. Sarah Finley's her name, and she's the niece of the partner he shot a couple days ago. Now that her uncle's dead, she owns half o' that mine, an' Porter is bound to do her out of it!"

Miss Birdie Boynton frowned. She did not appreciate having her own conclusions questioned. But what she heard bothered her. She stood before him, arms akimbo.

"I don't believe that's true," she said. "You sure you're not makin' all that up, Ed Musgrove? Just to soften me up?"

He raised a hand in mock oath-taking and rolled his eyes piously. "You don't hafta believe me! Go talk to Sarah Finley."

"Well," she mused, "Mr. Porter seems to me to be a purfick gentleman. An' besides, he owns a mine!"

"Yeah, an' that makes it all right with you, I s'pose!" "If they got money, that's all you dolls care about—"

"It ain't with me!" she flared. "I may work in a bar, but I got principles! I'm goin' to ask Al about that, an' if what you say is true, we got a little discussin' to do!"

Musgrove regarded her somewhat blearily and pointed a weaving finger. "That ain't all!" he said. "Maybe you ain't heard, but there's still a couple fellers down in that mine, and a lotta people think they're still alive. Sutro—the feller who's buildin' the drainage tunnel—says he offered to build a slope to the Nancy Belle to save those fellers an' that Porter turned him down cold. Porter won't spend a nickel to save those two so's he won't hafta pay Sutro his commission. Talk to your friend Al Porter about that, while you're at it!" he taunted.

He attempted to depart with dignity, an effect somewhat marred by his weaving gait. But he left the girl frowning in thought.

As Mr. Musgrove regained his table and referred again to the whiskey, Pat Flaherty rose from his chair and faced Al Porter across his littered desk.

"So you won't do nothin' to save them poor bhoys?" he repeated angrily.

"They're dead!" Porter said stubbornly.

"That ain't necessarily true," Flaherty insisted.

Porter stood up and thumped a heavy fist on his desk. "I ain't goin' to pay Sutro no two dollars a ton!" he roared. "What right has he got to talk to you—and everybody else —about what a son-of-a-bitch I am! He's just tryin' to line his own pockets! Even if I let him do it—which I ain't goin' to—it would take him so long to dig a shaft to our eight-hundred level that—"

Flaherty shook his head. "He wouldn't have to go to the eight-hundred-foot level. I been lookin' at his blueprints. If he connected down three drifts lower, it'd do it. All he needs is a winze, and not too long a one, either—"

Porter flushed with rage. "I ain't goin' to do it! That's final! Now get out of here!"

Flaherty left the office shaking his head, but he made his way to town and conversed with the marshal, a heavyset man who wore a black sombrero and a large badge.

"I'll go see Al," said the marshal. "But I don't know it'll do much good. He's a stubborn devil."

"Thanks, Tom," Flaherty said. "I got to do what I can fer them two bhoys—or I'll never sleep."

A little later that day the marshal knocked on the Nancy Belle's office door, and Porter grudgingly allowed him to enter.

For a time they talked, but as the marshal left, he repeated something he had gone over before.

"Remember, Al, I was willin' to overlook your shootin' of Grant Finley and not make nothin' of it, considerin' it as a fair fight. But Sutro's talkin' all over the place, and if you get a lot of public opinion riled up against you, I may not be able to ignore it. Better think about it."

As the door closed behind him, Porter swore vehemently. "Damn meddlin' bastards!" he exclaimed, picking up a fistful of papers from the desk and throwing them to the floor. "Sutro's doin' this! I wouldn't pay him a nickel no matter *what* happens!

Seething, he sat at his desk for a time, but when his pulse failed to slow, he decided he needed some distraction. Thrusting his hat on his head, he clumped out of the office, locked the door behind him, and made his way toward C Street and the Oriental, where he knew feminine companionship awaited.

Once there he sat down at a small table, motioned the barman to bring a bottle, took off his hat, and mopped his brow. The half-dark interior of the Oriental, cool and shadowy, suited his mood and partially settled his ruffled feelings. At the end of the bar he spotted Miss Birdie Boynton, who further distracted him from his troubles. Even as he saw her, she saw him and headed toward him, high red heels clicking determinedly.

Good, he thought. He really had made a conquest. She was even leaving another customer for him. This was what he needed: something to think about besides the Nancy Belle, and what might be going on at the eight-hundred level, and what people were saying about him behind his back. His heavy lips spread in a smile of welcome as she approached.

She did not smile. Instead she faced him soberly, pulled out the chair opposite, and seated herself, keeping her slim body erect and hostile.

"I'm glad to see you," he said, reaching out for her hand, a hand which she withdrew immediately. "I've had a rough day," he went on. But at that point he detected the stiffness in her manner. "What's wrong, Birdie? Somethin' eatin' you?"

"Yeah," she said, leaning over the table to face him directly. "I wanta ask you a few questions, Al, and I want straight answers—straight, that is, if you ever expect me to speak to you again."

He scowled. "Fer Pete's sake, what is it? I came here for a little fun—"

"A little's all you'll get from me if you don't answer me straight. When you beat up that travelin' salesman, was you tryin' to steal somethin' from your pardner's niece?"

"Whaddaya mean, steal something?"

"Just what I say. Accordin' to the drummer, he was tryin' to keep you from takin' some paper, or somethin', from that girl. Is that so, or ain't it? I can always ask her, remember!"

Al Porter clutched his brow in frustration. "You don't know the whole story!" he exclaimed. "Grant Finley and I was pardners. Grant's dead—"

"Yeah. You shot him."

"He woulda shot me otherwise!" Porter pleaded. "Anyways, he's dead and I'm the survivin' pardner. I own the mine. That gal, his niece, is tryin' to take it away from me!"

"Well, she ought to git somethin' out of it, hadn't she? He *was* her uncle!"

Porter downed a drink and mopped his sweaty forehead. "I don't know why!" he contended. "*I* was his pardner!"

Miss Birdie Boynton narrowed a shrewd eye and leaned forward. "Al Porter, are you tellin' me that that pardnership agreement says that whoever's left alive gits the whole thing?"

"I shorely am!"

He reached out a fat hand and for a second time groped for hers.

"Come on, Birdie!" he encouraged. "Be reasonable! Quit worryin' about business, and let's have some fun!"

"Before we have any more fun, Al Porter, I intend to talk to Sarah Finley. I may work in a saloon, but I got principles!"

The blond bar girl pushed back her chair and stood up. "I'm goin' to see Sarah," she announced, "and after that I'll decide whether or not we're goin' to be friends."

Porter watched her flounce away, then swore to himself as he poured another drink out of the half-empty bottle.

CHAPTER 17

AT the eight-hundred-foot level in the Nancy Belle, Don Warren, his cap lamp relit, struggled through the warm water, again plunging into the dark tunnel where water, reaching to its rocky ceiling, had halted them before. His brother was now almost a dead weight on his shoulders. Greg had been silent for several minutes and had even stopped moaning. Don knew that Greg was close to losing consciousness.

The water deepened as Don sloshed forward, and he prayed hard that it had gone down enough for them to make their way through the dip in the tunnel.

The water was up to his shoulders, and he paused to rest, almost fearful to take steps forward. Another disappointment would mean tragedy. His spirits rose as Greg's body, which had been motionless, now shifted slightly.

"Don," he muttered, "I feel pretty bad. You better leave me and try to make it yourself."

"Not on your life!" The loudness of Don's voice reverberated in the water-filled cavern. "Don't even think of such a thing! We're almost at the deep spot in this drift, and this time we're going to make it! This time we'll do it!"

"I hope so," Greg murmured weakly. "I hope so."

"We will!"

Don took a long breath and pushed forward into deepening water. He knew they had to do it this time, before Greg could lapse into a coma from which he would never awaken.

The water crept up to Don's chin, then to his mouth, and,

finally to his nostrils. The cap lamp shone ahead on the black gleaming surface of the water—and once again the rock ceiling joined it, and small waves lapped against the rocky barrier.

Don halted, holding his head high to keep his nose above water. The water had stopped subsiding. It no longer was going down. If he tried to swim underwater for—who knew how many feet or yards?—and then had to return if it proved too far, Greg would have drowned by the time they either reached safety or found it unattainable.

Cold panic clutched Don's stomach. Unless a miracle occurred, this would be their grave.

Birdie Boynton found Sarah Finley in the back room of Emma Nelson's cafe and launched into her case without preamble.

"I been told," she said, "that my friend Al Porter took somethin' away from you that he shouldn't have. I ain't goin' to be friends with him if he did, and I wanta know what really happened."

Sarah Finley roused herself from her gloomy contemplation and regarded the girl without interest.

A dance-hall girl, obviously, with brassy blond hair; a spangled, skimpy dress; bare arms and shoulders; slim legs, and small feet in red-heeled pumps. The girl had a face that was pretty in a hard way. She was the type of woman whom Sarah's upbringing had taught her to avoid, one of the soiled doves who were never spoken of in polite society.

So depressed was Sarah, however, that it seemed at the moment to make little difference with whom she talked, and the girl's statement, if it were to be believed, indicated that, at the very least, she had a conscience.

"My name's Miss Birdie Boynton," the girl began. "We ain't been formally intraduced, but I figured this was important enough to come to you direct."

Emma Nelson, sensing something important, came in from the lunch counter to listen.

"Mr. Porter may be a friend of yours," Sarah reflected, "but he's no friend of mine. If he had been, he wouldn't have come to my room and taken my uncle's copy of their partnership agreement."

"Did that agreement say that the mine they both owned now belongs to him?"

"Mr. Porter says it does."

"But does it? Only to him?"

Sarah lost patience. "I don't know! I haven't read it," she confessed. "For all I know, it does. But if it does, it seems to me very unfair. I think my uncle's heirs should be entitled to something. And I am his heir—his only heir."

"You haven't read it?" Birdie sounded incredulous. "You didn't read it when you had it?"

"No, I didn't. In the first place, I didn't even find it until there was trouble at the mine; and—I've had other things to think about."

"I know," said Birdie softly. "I heard you was kinda sweet on that Warren boy who's still down there."

Sarah turned to hide a tear. "Let's not talk about it! I've had nothing but misery and trouble since I've been here, and I'd like to forget the whole thing and go away somewhere."

Emma Nelson intervened. "Now, just hold yer hosses!" she advised. "If you own half o' that mine, you shouldn't be thinkin' of goin' anywhere! Besides, that Warren boy's goin' to be all right, you hear?"

Sarah shook her head and pressed a handkerchief to her lips. Her shoulders shook with sobs.

Birdie spoke up. "Would you like to know what that agreement really says?" she asked.

"Sure she would," Emma volunteered for Sarah. "We got to make it our business to find out what's in that agreement."

Birdie nodded decisively. "Well, I'll git Al Porter to show me that paper, and as soon as I know what's in it, I'll come and tell you. And if Al's lied to me, he can look for another acquaintance!"

Emma Nelson broke into a broad smile and encircled

Birdie's slim shoulders with a massive, friendly arm. "That's the best thing I've heard in a good many hours!" she chortled. "You hear that, dearie?" she asked, turning to Sarah. "We got ourselves a friend in the enemy camp!"

Sarah stopped sobbing and looked up at the dance-hall girl. "Thank you," Sarah said brokenly.

"Al's comin' over to see me tonight, and I'll git a look at it, never fear!" said Birdie.

Her small jaw set, Birdie clicked her pumps out of the restaurant, grim determination on her face.

Belden Ward arrived in Virginia City in time to note a short-skirted dance-hall girl stride purposefully down C Street, coming from the direction of Sun Mountain, and disappear between the bat wing doors of the Oriental Saloon. At another time he might have reacted with more interest, being a bachelor. But now he had serious problems on his mind. He jumped from the stage, gave money to the Whip—who gaped at the amount—and told him to take his luggage to the best hotel in town. Ward then hastened up the street, in the opposite direction from which the girl had come.

On the way he halted a red-shirted pedestrian who had trouble maintaining a straight course. "Where are the Nancy Belle and the Lone Star mines?" he demanded.

The pedestrian regarded him blearily. "Yer headed in the right direction, stranger. Straight up the hill. First buildin' on the right."

Hurrying on up the hill, he ignored the heavy dust which settled on his shiny boots and, panting, arrived at the Lone Star headquarters.

Two people were inside: a nervous-looking young man with a gold-rimmed pince-nez, seated at a desk near the door; and in the inner office, a large, muscular man ruffling through papers.

"I'm Belden Ward," he announced, "the new owner of this mine."

The young man he told it to appeared even more nervous

than he had before. "Mr. Steele, the foreman, is the one you want to see," the young man stammered.

As if on cue, the man in the inner office rose to meet Belden Ward.

"Come on in," Steele greeted. "I'm doin' my level best to put order into the Lone Star records. Cobden didn't have much of a knack at it." He smiled and regarded Ward with interest. "I've heard of you, sir. Mighty pleased to meet you."

Ward impatiently shook his proffered hand, "I want to know what's going on," he declared. "I've got two of my employees here in town, one working for you and another at the Nancy Belle—and in San Francisco there's word a drift war's going on."

"You're right, sir, there is!" Ben Steele settled back in his chair and filled in Belden Ward on everything that had happened, including the gossip that Al Porter had rejected Sutro's offer and that Al had pumped bullets from a long-barreled Colt into the body of his partner, Grant Finley.

Ward brushed aside the business information. "There are men still down in the mine?" he asked.

"All of ours are accounted for, except the one Cobden hired last, the straw boss. Name's Warren. Say"— he raised his brows—"could he be the one you sent?"

"Greg Warren! My God, yes! You say he's still down there?"

"He may not be dead," Steele assured. "But the chances are he is. He was shot by somebody from the Nancy Belle, my boys tell me, and was lyin' acrost the rocks in the hole between the two stopes. If he wasn't above water level, he's prob'ly drowned."

"Well, for God's sake, can't we go down to see?"

Steele shook his head decisively. "The drift and stope are both flooded. The way I told you, Sutro offered to connect his tunnel with a winze to the Nancy Belle, which would drain both mines, but Al Porter turned him down. I sure don't have any authority to commit Lone Star funds—unless you give it to me." He stopped and regarded Ward warily.

"Yes, yes! By all means! Go find Sutro and tell him to go

ahead! As fast as possible! I'll pay all costs and give him a profit besides! Go find him! I'm making you manager of this mine! Later we'll talk details. Now hustle!"

Steele grinned broadly. "You're the kind of feller I've been hopin' to work for all my life. Funny, we're in trouble—and this is the first time I've got lucky!"

Happily, Steele ran from the office, and Ward lost no time bursting out of the Lone Star office and climbing up the hill to the Nancy Belle's shack. Without hesitation he entered but found nobody there. Two desks in the outer office were vacant, and so were the two in the inner. Swearing to himself, he went outside and found the elevator operator.

"Anybody still down there?" he demanded. "Mine's flooded, I understand."

The man removed his cigar from his mouth and nodded. "Everything's goin' to hell around here, I reckon. One of our bosses shot the other, t' other night. Then we struck a hot spring. Now the mine's full o' hot water and we've lost two men."

"Two men?"

"Yeah. Abe Stilson, and a young feller they just hired. Warren's his name."

Belden Ward obviously was not a miner, and his clothing indicated that he had come from far more civilized surroundings. But the lurid profanity which burst from him upon hearing this news astonished even the elevator operator—and his ears were accustomed to language that would blister the soul of a sinner.

"Where's Porter?" Ward bellowed angrily. "Why the hell isn't he here on the job?"

The elevator operator dropped his stogie in the dust. "I dunno, mister. Look fer him downtown. I ain't his keeper."

Then, red-faced but calm as he watched Belden Ward stomp down the mountainside, raising angry puffs of dust with every step, the man picked up his cigar from the ground, cursed it, brushed the dust from it, and reinserted it into his mouth.

* * *

The warm wind from the desert rose with the setting sun, and it set awnings flapping and raised dust devils on C Street as darkness fell over Virginia City.

Al Porter, in a bad humor, made his way toward the Oriental. The whiskey he had consumed earlier in the day had not improved his disposition, nor had Miss Birdie Boynton's attitude. He had decided not to go back to the Nancy Belle office, as the sight of the elevator and its idle operator gave him uncomfortable thoughts about what was going on below in the flooded drifts. So he spent the afternoon in his room in a boardinghouse off C Street and, with the coming of darkness, decided to return to the Oriental to give Birdie Boynton another chance to cheer him up.

As he made his way past miners homeward bound—or seeking livelier diversion—the town marshal approached him. Porter looked for a way past the man, but it was too late to avoid him.

"Feller's lookin' for ye. Mad as hell. Name of Ward —Belden Ward. You know him?"

Porter swore. "I know *of* him. What does he want?"

"Don't know. But he's madder'n hell."

The marshal departed down the street, and Porter continued toward the saloon. He suspected that he knew the answer to his own question. Don Warren had worked for Belden Ward, and Don Warren was still down in the flooded mine.

At the table in the Oriental, Porter ordered a bottle and looked around for Birdie Boynton. She was not entertaining any of the other customers, nor was she in sight at the moment. But it still was early. Perhaps she had not yet arrived. He poured himself a drink and swallowed it glumly. When she did arrive, it probably would be with the same unfriendly attitude she had displayed earlier. Well, he—Al Porter—had the means to soften up any bar girl. He felt the coins in his pocket. He'd also picked up a little something for her—it was in a smaller box in his other pocket. He pulled it out and snapped open the box. The jeweled pin glittered in the gaslight.

She couldn't resist that.

But where was she? He downed two more drinks and became impatient. The evening crowd was gathering. Other bar girls appeared in their shabby finery. He noted with disgust a plaid-suited figure who entered—this time without a cane—and swaggered his way to the bar. Mr. Ed Musgrove caught a glimpse of Porter hunched over his table and dropped his swagger. He made his way to the bar at the far end of the room, as distant from Porter as possible.

At long last—way past nine o'clock, and after Porter had been waiting for the better part of two hours—Birdie entered and surveyed the room. Porter, having consumed half a bottle of powerful frontier whiskey by that time, which didn't dispose him to tolerate any foolishness, motioned her to join him.

She did so, and he was surprised to note that there was a smile on her face ·and no vestige of the hostility that had marked her demeanor on their previous encounter.

Porter did not rise to seat her, but he did pull out a chair beside him, and she seated herself. "Hi, Al," she greeted, archly adjusting her hair.

"You over yer grouch?" he asked. "Ready fer some fun?"

"Yeah," she replied carelessly. "I've been to see Sarah Finley, an' she never even read the paper Ed Musgrove was so excited about. If she ain't int'rested, I guess I ain't either."

That day Porter had not bothered to shave, and he spread his stubbly thick lips in a broad grin.

"Now you're talkin'!" he exclaimed. "What's a little white-faced ninny like her doin' out here in a man's country, anyhow? B'sides, with me ownin' all o' the Nancy Belle, you an' me can have some real fun, cutie. I promise you you won't be sorry!"

Birdie smiled coyly at him and snuggled a little closer. "You're the kinda feller I like, Al," she confided, batting her theatrical lashes at him. "A big minin' man an' willin' to spend a little of his prosperity on a girl."

Al Porter, led on by her kittenish mood, said something he never would have without the help of the bottle.

"I'll tell you somethin' nobody else knows, Birdie," he said, his solemn, bleary eyes confronting hers.

"Yeah? What is it, my big, strong, handsome man?"

He leaned closer, his whiskey breath in her face. She suppressed a grimace and gave him her best wide-eyed stare. "Nancy Belle's in bonanza again!" he whispered hoarsely in her ear. "In the biggest bonanza since Consolidated Virginia!" Triumphantly he leaned back in his chair. "Whatcha think of *that*?"

Birdie assumed a proper air of doglike admiration. "Gee, Al, you'll be rich!" was all she said. But she raised a slim, soft hand and stroked his stubbly face.

"I shorely will!" he bragged. "Now"—and he leaned forward again, conspiratorially—"don't tell nobody about it yet. I wanta get all my smelter contracts signed before anyone knows. If word leaks out that I'm in bonanza, Bill Sharon'll raise his rates. You're the only one who knows!"

He continued to squint at her. "Birdie," he said at last, tentatively, "how about you an' me goin' upstairs? I got ye a little present, just to celebrate. But I don't wanta haul it out in front of all these bums."

He sat back, waiting for her refusal, which had been forthcoming on every previous occasion he had made the same suggestion. But to his surprise, this time she smiled invitingly and said, "Ooh! A present! What could it be?"

"Upstairs?" He raised his brows questioningly.

In reply, she rose and moved toward the end of the bar, where the stairway to the private rooms was located. But at the foot of the stairs, she halted and faced him.

"Al, you don't happen to have that pardnership agreement with you, do you?" she asked. "As far as I'm concerned, Sarah Finley can go peddle her papers—but I did promise to look at it, an' I like to keep my word."

Porter scowled. "I got it right here," he said, patting his coat pocket. "An' I ain't lettin' it outa my sight until things has settled down. But whatta you want to see it for? If I own the Nancy Belle all by myself, you're goin' to be gettin' a lotta presents from me. If I don't, things ain't goin' to be so friendly.

Birdie, coming close again to Porter, took the lapels of his coat in her hands and smiled up into his big, heavy face. Her perfume, not by any means the most delicate scent, was heady in his nostrils. Batting her eyelashes at him, she wheedled, "Now, Al, you know me. I wouldn't care if that paper said Sarah Finley owned the whole mine! You don't think I'd tell her about that, do you? I'm a businessgirl. She ain't disposed to give me presents—and you are. With you ownin' the whole mine, I got a bright future. It's just for my own satisfaction that I'd like to know what that paper says."

His scowl deepened. "Why, Birdie? If you feel the way you say, why should you know?"

"Look, Al," she said impatiently, "You've had a few drinks, an' you ain't thinkin' clear. Sarah's goin' to be seein' me in town sometimes, even if I don't look her up, an' she's goin' to ask, 'Did you see the paper?' If I say, 'No,' she'll go after the marshal or somebody to git you to show it. There's a lotta talk in town about you, you know, shootin' yer pardner and all. But if I tell her, 'Yes, I seen it, an' it gives the whole shootin' match to Al Porter,' why, then, she'll give up, 'cuz she'll believe me. Don't you see that?"

He scratched his head. "I guess so," he said. "You could turn her off."

"But only if I tell her I've seen the paper. You see that, don't you?"

"I suppose so." Still, he was reluctant. "All right, I'll let you see it. But first let's go upstairs and I'll give ye yer present."

Upstairs in the Oriental were three rooms, furnished in red plush with mirrors, following the model of a famous San Francisco restaurant. Each room had a door which bolted from the inside. Birdie and Al Porter entered one of the rooms, and a barkeep followed on their heels, carrying a bottle of champagne in an ice bucket. The man set it down and stuck out a hand under Porter's nose. "Twenty bucks, pard," he said.

Grumbling, Porter paid it—but still the man stood there, hand outstretched.

"Them stairs is awful hard to climb, pard," he groaned meaningfully.

So Porter slapped a dollar into his hand, and the man sniffed—but accepted it—and left the room. Alone at last, Porter moved to the door, closed it, and turned the bolt.

"Now," he reached for the girl, "let's be friendly!"

But she wriggled out of his grasp. "How about the present?" she asked.

"Oh, yeah, the present." Fumbling with uncertain fingers, Porter pulled the small box out of his pocket and snapped open the lid.

"Ooh!" she gasped—and ran with it to the gaslight. "How pretty!" she gushed. "It musta cost a bundle, Al!"

"I ain't cheap—an' I ain't goin' to be when it comes to you."

"Gee, Al, thanks! It's real pretty!" She stood on tiptoe and gave him a pecking kiss. He reached for her again, but again she eluded his grasp.

"How about that paper, Al? Let's see it an' git that outa the way. Then we'll have fun."

He frowned suspiciously. "Naw, let's do that later. Come on, I've waited long enough! I bought you a present an' paid through the nose for a bottle o' champagne which I didn't want. Now let's enjoy ourselves—"

He removed his coat and threw it on the bed.

Birdie's face and voice hardened. "No, Al," she said firmly. "There won't be no fun an' games until I see that paper. Now, git that through yer bean! I made a promise, an' I keep my word!"

He reached again, but this time she slapped his hand sharply.

He swore, prompted by frustration and pain, and went to his coat lying on the bed.

The same second, Birdie took a swift step toward the door, unlatching the bolt while his attention was concentrated on taking the paper from the inside pocket of his coat. This done, she stepped back to face him.

He handed the paper to her. "It'll take ye a while to read it," he said. "It ain't short."

"That's all right with me. I got the evening."

She seated herself on the single chair in the room and started to read.

He crouched on the edge of the bed, drumming his fingers on his knee impatiently for a while, then struggled with the champagne cork, which popped out, struck the ceiling, and bounced to the floor.

Finally she raised her head. "I don't understand all these big words," she said, "but this sounds pretty clear to me:

> In the event of the death of one of the partners, that partner's share of the mining stock shall go to his designated heirs. And in the event there are no heirs, the court shall decide—with the preponderance of the right to the claim going to the surviving partner.

"Sarah is Grant Finley's heir. So you really don't own all of the Nancy Belle, do you, Al?"

Porter rose and, with an ugly snarl, snatched the paper from her. "I've shown you the paper, and now you'd damned well better tell Sarah what you said you'd tell her! Come here! I'm tired waitin'!"

He moved toward her, his eyes glazed on her creamy shoulders and arms and on the pretty, regular features of her hard little face.

Anticipating his move, she leaped to her feet and opened the unbolted door.

"Sorry, Al," she said, smiling. "I not only keep my word, I also got some principles. An' not havin' fun with killers and thieves is one of 'em."

Slipping quickly through the doorway, she slammed the door in his face.

*   *   *

Ben Steele hurried to the little wooden office which bore the label, SUTRO TUNNEL HEADQUARTERS, Adolf Sutro, Prop. Inside he found the German engineer poring over blueprints with his foreman.

"*Der* vinze," he was saying, "goes oop from this level *und* reaches the t'ousand-foot level of Lone Star. Dis vill drain both Lone Star *und* Nancy Belle."

Ben Steele overheard. "You're doing it?" he demanded. "Where'd you get the money?"

"Ah, Mr. Steele!" Sutro rose and shook hands. "*Ja*, I am doing it—because I am a humane man *und* because I vish to show Mr. Porter dot he cannot condemn a man to death. But—*Geld?* I do not know. I haf none for this." He shrugged. "*Gott* vill provide. It iss a goot cause."

Ben Steele grinned. "I'm here to provide it. I'm commissioned by Belden Ward, my new boss, to tell you to go ahead at his expense. And you can name a profit."

Sutro gripped Steele by the arms and broke into loud laughter. "I said *Gott* vill provide! He has! But as to profit—*nein!* I vant no profit! My expenses, yes! Now we can go mit three shifts! *Gut* " He turned back toward his foreman. "You hear dot? Hurry! Efery minute counts!"

The man hastened out of the office with the blueprints under his arm, and Sutro motioned Steele to a chair.

"Tell me about Belden Ward," he urged. "I haf heard of him. But not that he has bought the Lone Star."

So Steele told him of Ward's arrival and of the incident which had brought about his own promotion.

"Congratulations!" Sutro exclaimed, his interest in Belden Ward as great as Steele's. "*Und* he iss a humane man, I am glad to know. Not like dot *Schweinhund* Porter!"

"The Warren boys are brothers," Steele mused. "They may not have known it, but they got into the drift war on opposite sides. Strange that they're the two left underground!"

Sutro shook his head in sympathy. "There iss a chance that they are still alife—but ve must hurry! Ve must hurry!"

* * *

Birdie Boynton hastened down the street toward Emma Nelson's cafe. Birdie looked fearfully over her shoulder from time to time as she hurried, bumping into people occasionally and failing to beg their pardon. Al Porter, after all, was no one to tangle with when he was fighting drunk. And Birdie knew that Al would willingly kill her.

She reached the cafe and rounded the counter into the back room, where she found both Emma and Sarah Finley.

"Did ye get a look at it?" Emma demanded.

Birdie tried to catch her breath, and after a moment, she nodded vehemently.

"I saw it," she said. "And it says half the mine belongs to—you!" She pointed at Sarah.

"There!" Emma chortled, her many chins bouncing with satisfaction. "I told ye! You're a rich girl! You're a mine owner! But now," she said, frowning, "if'n we don't git that paper away from Al Porter, he's li'ble to burn it, so's there's no record!"

"But Birdie could be a witness in court!" Sarah said. "She's seen it. And don't they file partnership agreements like that with the government offices? Especially mining claims? I saw some when I was at the Nancy Belle office—"

"The pardners would file a claim," said Emma darkly. "But that filin' wouldn't necessarily say anythin' about what happened to the claim in case one o' the pardners kicked off. No, we got to git that paper somehow!"

"But how," Sarah demanded, "if Birdie couldn't get it away from him? And Birdie, I want to say how grateful I am for what you did. Thank you, thank you with all my heart! It took courage and—conscience. You have them both!"

"Well, I may not be a member o' high society," Birdie said, "but I got an idea o' right an' wrong. And that Al Porter is a bum, just an ordinary bum! But how are we goin' to get that paper back? I'm sorry I let him snatch it away from me. I wasn't expectin' it."

"Don't blame yourself, dearie," Emma said. "You done very well. We just got to figure how to take the next step."

There was silence as the three cogitated.

Then Birdie said, "There's another feller who's int'rested in me. I might get him to do somethin'."

"I don't want you to use your friends, Birdie," Sarah said. "You've done enough."

"Now, just hold yer hosses!" Emma put in. "If Birdie's got another beau who's lookin' to do her a favor, let's not ignore it! Who is the lucky feller?" she asked the girl.

"Ed Musgrove, the drummer," said Birdie. "Al Porter's caned him already, so I know he's scared of Al. But he's the only one I can think of. And he might try. Al's mad at me now—but a girl can have second thoughts, can't she? If Ed just happened to be standin' outside the window of the Oriental tomorrow night in that little alley, he might be able to pick up somethin' I could toss out. It could work—if I can soften up Al again."

"But that could be dangerous for you!" Sarah protested. "How are you going to get it away from him?"

Birdie arched her brows. "He keeps it in his inside coat pocket. I seen it there. And one o' the first things fellers do in that upstairs room is take off their coat. Another thing they do is git kinda distracted. They don't pay much attention to anythin' but what they're concentratin' on." She whirled around to Sarah. "I know you're shocked, but if we can do somethin' good by doin' somethin' bad, then maybe what we're doin' ain't so bad after all!"

"I can't have you do that!" Sarah insisted. "It would lead to dirty money—"

Emma moved her ponderous bulk between the two. "*No* money is dirty, dearie, if it's used right. And you're the kind who'd use it right. What would be dirty would be for Al Porter to keep somethin' that isn't his'n an' put it to foul uses. Ain't that right, dearie?" she appealed to Birdie. "Besides, now that I'm gittin' to know you better, what I see don't strike me as bad atall. Not atall!" She put her hands on her hips and turned to Sarah. "Now, you listen to reason, dearie. This little girl an' I will organize everythin'—an' it'll come out fine! I meself will find Mr. Musgrove, with his checked pants, an' Birdie will tell me what to tell him!"

Sarah, too troubled to speak, sat looking straight ahead. But Emma and Birdie paid no heed to her as they put their heads together.

In the gloomy drift at the eight-hundred level, Don Warren shifted his brother's weight on his shoulders and tried to swallow his panic.

The flooded low point of the tunnel which led to the shaft might not have prevented him, if he had been alone, from swimming underwater for a few yards and coming up at the higher level beyond. But carrying his wounded brother, such a swim would be impossible. Greg, half conscious now, would choke and drown even if Don were able to drag him the indeterminate distance.

And the distance itself was a problem. If it turned out to be too far, even for Don—then to find oneself underwater in a totally stygian cavern, with a mountain of rock above one's head and without enough breath to return to the air-filled stope was frightening even to think about.

Don's jaw tightened. In the thin beam of his candle cap, he checked the water level against the same rock point he had checked it against earlier. Again his heart sank. It had not receded a fraction of an inch.

Greg shifted painfully on his shoulders. "Are we—are we goin' to try to get through?" he asked.

Don Warren took a deep breath and forced himself to lie. "The water's goin' down, Greg boy. We'll wait just a few more minutes—"

"I—I don't think we'd better," Greg gasped. "I feel terrible. My head's spinning. I—I—"

His shaky, weak voice gave out, and Don felt his brother's

head fall limply forward. Without looking, he knew his brother was unconscious.

Standing there in the warm water, Don Warren, for the first time in his life, knew what it was to be utterly hopeless.

Even with a crew from the surface there was little chance of draining the tunnel from the shaft end. It wouldn't work. He remembered distinctly that the drift rose rapidly just before it reached the elevator.

He and Greg were doomed. By the time anything were done—even if by some miracle Sutro got into it—the chances were it would be too late. If not for him, at any rate for Greg, who even now lay like a dead man across his shoulders.

Dispiritedly, hopelessly, his stomach churning with fear, Don turned, bent on slogging and slushing his way back toward the stope, where they could at least sit on the rough cribbing and start to dry off.

A new fear clutched him. How long could the wall sconce last? Dying was one thing. But dying in absolute darkness, eight-hundred feet under a mountain, was another.

He pushed slowly forward. Ahead of him gleamed the dim, flickering reflection of the single remaining sconce, its light making eerie the oily surface of the water-filled cavern.

He shifted the burden of Greg's limp body on his shoulders. Greg, he thought, was luckier than he. He no longer knew what it was to be doomed without hope of salvation.

CHAPTER 18

"I ain't so sure." The drummer shook his head pessimistically. "I tangled with that bruiser once already, an' I didn't come out so good."

Emma Nelson leaned over her counter and watched as Mr. Musgrove consumed the last large bite of a free piece of apple pie from her cafe icebox.

"Listen!" she said. "You ain't even goin' to *see* Al Porter! All you got to do is stand outside that winda in the alley beside the Oriental an' pick up what Birdie throws out. Then run. Al won't even know somethin's been thrown out the winda. An' even if he does, he won't know who picked it up. All he'll see—if he sees you, which he won't— will be somebody runnin' in the dark."

"An' what if he's got a gun?"

"Well, it's only a few steps around the corner of the buildin', an' no gun will shoot around corners! Here, have another piece o' pie!"

Mr. Musgrove was pensive as he accepted it and took another large bite. "I ain't anxious to tangle with Al Porter," he said with his mouth full.

Emma watched him eat. The pie disappeared in a hurry, Mr. Musgrove being one of those who favored large mouthfuls and rapid consumption of anything tasty.

"If you ever want to see Birdie Boynton again, you'll do it!" Emma told him. "B'sides, ain't Sarah Finley worth doin' somethin' for?"

Mr. Musgrove sat back and picked his teeth reflectively. "You say Birdie wants me to do this?"

"She tole me," Emma lied, rolling her eyes. " 'Tell Ed Musgrove I'll be ferever grateful if he'll do this,' she said. Now, I'd do it myself," Emma went on, "but folks in town know how I feel about saloons—an' if I was caught lurkin' in the alley beside the Oriental, it'd cause comment. An' with my size, I'd be sure to be caught."

"Yeah," said Mr. Musgrove, eyeing Emma's bulk across the counter. "Yeah, you're right about that. You sure about Birdie sayin' she'd be appreciative if I'd do this?"

"Heaven fergive me," Emma muttered to herself as she crossed her fat fingers behind her back. Aloud she said to Mr. Musgrove, her fingers still crossed, "So help me, Birdie'll be yer friend fer life if you do this favor fer her now."

"How could she consider it a favor for *her*?" Mr. Musgrove asked, looking perplexed. "It seems like a favor for Sarah Finley."

Emma nodded solemnly. "Well, it is. But Birdie looks on this as her duty, an' she likes Sarah an' thinks she's gettin' a raw deal. Birdie's signed up, I tell ya. She wants this to work!"

"I think Sarah Finley's gettin' a raw deal too. But I don't intend to git killed jest because I feel sorry fer her. Still"—he hesitated, musing aloud a solution—"if everything's as you say it is—in the dark alley an' all, an' it's likely he won't see me—why, then—"

"I knowed you'd do the right thing!" Emma interrupted, straightening up and thrusting out a massive hand, which Mr. Musgrove shook. "How about cinchin' the deal with another piece o' apple pie?"

"Well," said Mr. Musgrove thoughtfully, "if you put it that way, I might consider it."

Herr Adolf Sutro made his way, panting, up the slope of Sun Mountain toward the Lone Star administration shed. His long coat flared out behind him, and dust rose from each step he took. Red-faced, he burst into the office of the Lone Star and stood, palms flat against the wall behind him, trying to regain his composure.

Ben Steele, conscious of his authority as the new manager, sprang from his desk to greet him.

"Mr. Sutro!" he exclaimed. "What's wrong?"

"*Der* vinze!" Sutro panted. "Ve haf struck hard rock! It vill not be easy! It vill not be fast! Ve may not be able to do it in *der* vay I intended!"

A second man came from within the Lone Star office. He was short, stocky, gray-haired, square-faced, and grim. He strode directly to the other. "Mr. Sutro?" he queried. "I'm Belden Ward. I'm paying for your winze."

Sutro, having recovered his breath, came forward. "I am happy to meet you, sir," he said. "And even more happy to meet a Christian gentleman who iss humane and vants to safe human life. But I haf bad news. *Der* vinze dot I planned to a lower level of *der* Lone Star—it iss blocked by lava rock. Most difficult *und* slow to penetrate—"

Ward thrust his face into Sutro's. "Are you telling me there's no way to rescue those boys?"

"But yes! If I could send der vinze forty-fife degrees at an angle east *und* get to der t'ousand-foot level of der Nancy Belle—perhaps *der* rock iss soft. Perhaps ve could make it!"

"Well, why the hell don't you go in that direction then?" Ward demanded.

Sutro shrugged and spread his hands. "De owner of *der* Nancy Belle vill not permit!"

"Porter won't permit? When there are lives to be saved?"

"He vill not! I haf asked him."

Ward, purple-faced, looked to Ben Steele. "What kind of a curmudgeon is this Al Porter? In all this trouble he hasn't been around all day. Is he a worm?"

Steele nodded silently.

"He's a son-of-a-bitch, then, is that it?" Ward demanded.

Steele's head continued to bob affirmatively, and when

Ward looked to Sutro for confirmation, the German engineer nodded agreement.

Ward squared his shoulders. "Well, I'll find Al Porter—and I'll make him listen to reason! Where can I find him?"

Sutro shrugged. "They say he spends much time in *der* saloon—*der* Oriental."

"And he lives just off C Street," Steele offered. "I know where it is."

"You direct me," Ward ordered. "But first I'll try the saloon." His eyes steely hard, he turned to Sutro. "Whatever Porter has told you, you start moving toward the Nancy Belle's thousand-foot level."

Sutro shook his head. "Sir," he said, wringing his hands, "I haf run into so much trouble *mit* politicians *und* odders, dot I cannot do it mitout permission."

Ward jutted his square jaw. "Then, by God, I'll find Porter and *make* him give permission!"

Heels thumping, Belden Ward strode out of the office.

The mining engineer looked after him. "Vot I vish him is luck!" he told Steele and clasped his hands.

CHAPTER 19

AS darkness fell over Virginia City, activity in Emma Nelson's cafe increased. Sarah Finley arrived from her room with a sad and sober mien. Emma attempted to cheer her.

"This is goin' to work, dearie!" she assured. "We'll get that paper, and by that time that Dutchman's tunnel will have drained the Nancy Belle, and your young man'll be back with you!"

Sarah looked up at her and shook her head. "I wish you wouldn't talk that way, Emma," she said. "You know as well as I do that Don is dead. Keeping up my hopes will make it even harder when they bring up his body—if they ever do."

Emma threw up her hands and rolled her eyes. "I dunno what it takes to make you see facts! Really, dearie, you're altogether too gloomy! Things ain't that bad! Now, let's organize this chivaree tonight so's it will work without a hitch!" She stomped over to the window. "Where in hell's that drummer? He said he'd be here by this time."

The words were barely out of her mouth when the door swung open and Mr. Musgrove stood on the threshold. He was gloriously drunk, and weaving.

"Here I am, ladies!" he called, waving his cane and gripping the doorjamb with his other hand. "Ready for action! But I don't see Porter—"

Emma, flushed with rage, hurried over to him and yanked him to a chair. "Listen, you!" she hissed. "This wasn't the night fer you to git stinkin'! An' you better shake yerself sober damn quick!"

Seated in the chair and trying to keep his tongue flexible enough for speech, Mr. Musgrove drew himself up indignantly. "Who's drunk? If you're referrin' to me, I'm sober as a—judge."

Emma took him by his shoulders and shook him like a terrier. "Listen, you!" she said again. "I'm goin' to pour a gallon o' coffee in you, an' you're goin' to walk the floor here until you sober up—at the very least, until Birdie comes! Now, git up outa that chair—"

Sarah was even more depressed than Emma when she saw the salesman. "It's never going to work," Sarah protested. "Let's forget the whole thing."

"Nothing doing!" Emma was busy jamming a full coffee cup under Mr. Musgrove's nose. "Now, drink up, ye spalpeen! Ye've drunk enough other stuff! Drink this!"

Mr. Musgrove sputtered, half choked, and drank. Emma then took him by the hand and walked him briskly around the room. This went on for nearly an hour. Then Birdie entered.

Emma looked back, glared at Mr. Musgrove, and nodded. "We're as ready as we're goin' to be, dearie," she said. Birdie turned on her heel and left, and Emma turned to Mr. Musgrove. Her eyes were dangerous. "Now!" she ordered, menacingly. "You do what ye agreed to do—an' do it right, mind ye—or ye'll answer to me! An' what'll be left when I git through with ye won't be worth fixin'!"

Mr. Musgrove, who was considerably more sober than he had been when he entered, gazed fearfully upon the large woman towering over him.

"Have no fear, ladies!" he assured with dignity, the dignity marred somewhat by a hiccup. "I will perform in my usual effective manner!"

And with that he teetered from the room, swinging the cane from his arm.

Emma watched him leave, arms akimbo. "That fancy-pants better do it right," she seethed, "or Grant Finley won't be the only one to be buried this week!"

In the Oriental, Al Porter sat at a table in the shadows. Why he had come here after Birdie had rejected him, he did not know. But here he was. A killer and a thief, she'd called him. No woman could call him that and get away with it! He was on the verge of becoming one of the richest men in the Comstock. Him! Al Porter, who had just maneuvered himself into control of another bonanza that would make the Gould & Currys and the Yellow Jackets and the Crown Points, look like a handful of counterfeit Mexican *centavos*. Birdie had rejected *him*! *That* was why he was here—to tell that cheap little trollop what he thought of her and to get back the pin he'd given her. Why the hell should she keep that after what she'd said to him?

He'd been smart! You bet yer boots he'd been smart! He'd kept his stupid pardner from knowing what was going on, and when he finally found out, he'd put him out of the way. He'd made a deal with Cobden that had gotten him everything he'd wanted. And, by God, he'd even pulled the wool over Sharon's eyes! Sharon, the smartest man on the Comstock, the one everybody feared.

His only failure—and here he frowned again and felt uncomfortable—was with this little snip of a dance-hall girl. And tonight he was going to correct that. When she knew how really rich he was going to be, she'd think twice! You bet she would.

And there she was! Entering between the batwing doors the way she always did, head held high, looking neither right nor left.

But Birdie *was* looking, and when she saw Al Porter she took a long breath of relief. Her course now was clear. Pretending she did not see him, she went to the bar, and there she began a chatty conversation with the bartender. When finally she turned and surveyed the room, she allowed her eyes to fall on Porter.

He was glaring at her fixedly, and she knew he had been watching her ever since she arrived. Casually, and with affected nonchalance, she strolled, hips swaying, to his table.

"Hi, Al!" she greeted him. "Back again?"

He half rose from his chair. "Yeah," he said grimly. "And, Birdie, you just sit right down here, 'cause we're goin' to have a talk. You said some mighty hard words to me the other night, an' I wanta straighten a few things out!"

Birdie shrugged. "What makes you so sure I want to?" she asked. But as she spoke, she eased herself into the seat beside him. From that point on, she felt, things probably would go reasonably well.

CHAPTER 20

AT the eight-hundred level, in the flickering gloom of the single wall sconce, Don Warren regarded the inert form of his unconscious brother, whom he was holding, balanced against one of the rough beams of the stope cribbing.

Greg was dying, and a troublesome thought rose in Don's mind. He fought it at first, then surrendered to it.

If his brother were dying, should he sacrifice himself to save a corpse? Was it fair?

Angrily he put the thought from his mind. Greg was not dead, and in any case he would not desert his brother. Yet as he looked at Greg's motionless body and listened to his gasping, uneven breathing, the thought—evil and selfish as it was—kept recurring in his mind.

Don knew he had the strength to swim underwater the few yards he believed to be the only barrier to the elevator shaft. Of course, it might be farther than he thought, and if it were too far, he would drown. But he would have a chance at life, and it would be better than waiting to suffocate in the darkness.

As for Greg, he had done all he could to save him. It wasn't fair for one life to be sacrificed for one that already was lost.

For an hour or more, Don had all he could do to prevent the cold lump of panic from rising in his throat. And the more he thought, the more he became convinced that that underwater barrier was not long enough to keep him from saving himself. Now what he wanted more than anything else was to wade frantically into the tunnel and plunge into the flooded drift.

He could imagine himself surfacing on the other side, with the blessed elevator shaft ahead. He would be saved. And above the shaft was Sarah Finley, and the desert sunshine, and many years of life and happiness.

He had to swallow hard to keep from screaming, to keep the panic down below his throat.

He had done his best to save his brother, but his best had not been good enough. He leaned over Greg and adjusted his body on the beam so he would not roll off into the black water. Then Don slid off the cribbing.

The water came up to his chin, and he pushed heavily toward the drift. He did not look back. He knew if he did, he might not be able to carry out his determination.

The black hole of the tunnel entrance loomed before him. He paused before it. He remembered Greg when they both had been boys, playing together, getting along much better than most brothers. There had been affection and respect between them. Greg always had looked up to him, always had let him lead. Don remembered how Greg had defended him when he had been unjustly accused of breaking a window with a baseball.

Now he was deserting his brother. Worse, Greg was doomed because he, Don, had shot him. Shot his own brother! and he was leaving him to die.

Behind him Greg moaned softly. Don tried to ignore it, to look at the black entrance to the drift. It was his hope of life and hope and safety. His every nerve and muscle strained to push him forward for his chance at life. He advanced two more steps.

Then he stopped.

He could not desert his brother, even if that decision did doom them both to a horrible death. He swallowed, choked, and groaned aloud. It was not in him.

Slowly, sadly, but resolutely, he turned and waded through the warm, sulfurous water back to the beam where his brother lay.

* * *

Birdie was right. Most of the guests in the upper rooms removed their coats right away. And as Al Porter tossed his on the bed, Birdie saw the paper he had shown her the previous evening protruding from his inside pocket.

Porter reached out a lustful hand for her, but she had anticipated him and began to fan herself. "It's hot in here," she complained. "Open the winda." Willing to oblige her, Al did so, and as his back was turned, Birdie snatched the paper from his coat and followed him to the window. As he turned away from the sash, she pivoted in front of it and stood with her back to the opening. "Thanks, Al," she said, and —unbeknownst to him—the paper left her hand and fluttered to the surface of the alley.

"Now," said Al, "you been puttin' me off too long. I guess that at last you've seen the light and are willin' to be frien'ly with a rich man! So let's have some fun!"

Birdie sighed. She hoped that the paper was the right one and that it had reached the alley safely and—even more—that Ed Musgrove had been there to pick it up.

The sound of running feet below the window reassured her.

Again she sighed. "Okay, Al," she said, "let's have some fun."

An hour later, someone knocked loudly at the door of the upstairs room.

"Go 'way," Porter muttered. But Birdie sprang up to answer it. The bartender stood there, wiping his hands on his soggy apron.

"Feller lookin' fer you, Mr. Porter," he said over Birdie's shoulder.

"Well, tell him to go drown himself!" Porter grated. "Tell him I'll see him tomorra."

The bartender shook his head. "He ain't of a mood to go, Al. Name's Belden Ward. He seemed pretty interested to be sure you know that. An' he's loaded for bear!"

Porter scratched his head. "Has he got a gun?" he asked.

"No gun. But he's mad as hell and seems to be kinda important. Bill Sharon was in this afternoon—just to leave word that if Ward came in, he'd like to see him."

"Hell!" Porter groaned and rose from the bed, straightened his collar, pulled up his somewhat ragged string tie, smoothed his hair, and reached for his coat. Automatically he patted the inside pocket. Then his face froze. He suddenly swore, scrambled out of the coat, searched frantically in each of its pockets, looked quickly at the rumpled bed, and got down on his knees to search the floor under it. When he rose, his face was purple and he was breathing fire.

"Birdie!" he roared. "Where the hell's that agreement?"

He could see that she was attempting to slip out of the room past the bartender, but he was too quick for her. Cruelly he seized her by the arm and jerked her to his side.

"Where is it?" he demanded hoarsely. "You took it, didn't you? I want it *now*!"

Birdie was frightened, but not too frightened to stick out her chin. "You'll never git it back, Al Porter!" she taunted. "By now, Sarah Finley's got it!"

He growled with rage, shook her like a terrier, let go of her arm, and took a full-armed swing with his fist. It smashed against her jaw, lifted her from the floor, and crashed her against the wall, where she lay silently.

"Now, wait, fer goshsakes—" The bartender attempted to intervene but shrank back when he saw the depth of Porter's rage. Porter couldn't care less; he slammed out of the room and pounded down the stairs.

"Golly!" the barman muttered as he bent over the unconscious girl. "I hope he didn't break her neck."

Below, in the saloon, Porter hastened toward the batwings which led to the street, but before he reached them, a square-faced, solid figure barred his way.

"You're Al Porter?" the man queried.

Porter was tempted to use the same tactics on Ward that he

had used on Birdie, but was alert enough, despite his anger, to realize that now, without the partnership agreement, it might be wise not to make another powerful enemy.

He halted, panting and red-faced. "I'm Porter," he acknowledged. "What do you want?"

"I want to talk," said Ward brusquely. "I want permission—and I want it *now*—for Sutro to drive a winze up to your thousand level so we can save the lives of whoever's left in that mine."

Porter was still sizzling. "Well, you can't have it!" he barked. "I don't intend to mortgage my soul to Adolf Sutro, with his damned two-dollar-a-ton rakeoff! Forget it—and get out of my way!"

Ward did not move. "I don't intend to forget it!" he said bluntly. "I want that permission—and not a week from Sunday either—and I'll get it, one way or another." He regarded Porter sharply, saw he was too angry to be rational. "I hear you've borrowed from Bill Sharon for some purpose or other. Let me tell you, Sharon's a friend of mine. I'll see what I can do from that end. But whether you like it or not, I'm going to get that permission—and I'm going to get it fast!"

He swung on his heel and left the saloon. Porter just stood there, red-faced with anger, chest heaving. He knew he'd borrowed from Sharon on the understanding that the mine was all his. Porter slammed out of the Oriental, a blue blaze of profanity coming from his lips. He must find Sarah Finley and *quickly*.

CHAPTER 21

IT was ten o'clock in the evening, but seeing a light in Sharon's office, Belden Ward entered and pounded on the inner door.

Sharon himself answered the door, frowning, but when he saw Ward, he removed the long cigar from between his lips and grinned.

"Belden!" he greeted. "I've been looking for you. Come in." A fine host, he led the way into his inner office, with its Victorian luxury.

"I've been looking for you, too, Bill," said Ward. "But we haven't got time for the amenities. Two of my boys are stuck down in that flood in the Lone Star and the Nancy Belle—and I want to get 'em out."

"You think they're still alive?" Sharon asked. "I hear Porter wouldn't let Sutro drain the works."

"But it's supposed to be a big stope, with a lot of air. They've got a chance if we get to 'em—fast!"

Sharon regarded his cigar carefully. "It's probably too late, but what can I do to help?"

"They say you loaned Al Porter a bundle."

Sharon nodded. "It was a queer deal," he said. He needed a survey to prove that the Nancy Belle had a claim to bonanza ore that Lone Star thought it owned. With Finley dead—and on the basis that Al now was sole owner of the Nancy Belle—I made him a loan to finance it."

Ward stroked his chin. "Sutro won't move without Porter's

approval," he said. "I've got to figure out a way to put pressure on him to give it."

"How can I help?" Sharon asked.

"You could recall the loan."

"On what basis? It was a straight deal, under certain conditions."

Ward's eyes narrowed. "Porter had a partner named Finley?" he asked.

"Right. The one he shot in a squabble the other day."

"Isn't there some law that says that if one partner kills another, there's a shadow on his claim?"

Sharon rolled back his head and laughed. "Back in civilization, maybe. But not here. The marshal's already cleared Al on that. Self-defense. No problem."

"Didn't Finley have any heirs?"

"He's got a niece. He brought her here and she worked for him. But he assured me that the partnership agreement left him in full control."

"I'd like to see Sarah Finley," Belden Ward advised.

"Well, she's got a room somewhere in Virginia City—and I've seen her a couple of times with Emma Nelson, that big, fat woman who runs a cafe just off C Street. Why don't you ask Emma?"

"How do I get to that restaurant?" Ward asked.

Al Porter didn't need any directions to find the place where Sarah Finley lived, and he hastened through the darkness, down the slope off C Street, toward the boardinghouse.

The windows were dark, but he pounded on the door of a first-floor room anyway, and when a sleepy, tousled miner in a wrinkled nightshirt came angrily to the door, Porter demanded to know which room Sarah occupied.

At first the man was irritated enough to refuse a reply, but Porter's glaring eyes, clenched fists, and threatening manner changed his mind.

Porter thundered up the stairs and pounded on the door. There was no answer, but he had no intention of letting that stop him. Growling with rage, he backed across the hall and hurled the full force of his body against the door, which obliged by splintering open.

The room was empty. Fumbling for a match in his pocket, he lit a candle on the table and began a hasty search through the neatly arranged dresser drawers and under the bed— wherever a girl might have hidden an important document.

The agreement was not there. He had to conclude that Sarah Finley was taking no chances.

He then bolted down the stairs, where the nightshirted miner still stood, open-mouthed, in the hall. Storming through the doorway, Porter headed back to the Oriental.

There he found additional turmoil. The usual card games had ceased, and the bar loungers were crowded on the staircase.

Undaunted, he pushed his way toward the stairs—until someone saw him and identified him.

"Here's the scalawag who hurt Birdie!" the man yelled. "Get him!"

The saloon crowd, with a menacing roar, turned its attention from the upstairs room and half scrambled, half fell down the staircase in its rush toward him.

Porter had intended to extract further information from Birdie as to Sarah Finley's whereabouts, but he had not anticipated this. He took one quick look at the angry, bearded faces, heard the oaths and shouts of rage, recognizing it as an incipient lynch mob, and ran out into the street. He dodged into a passageway between two buildings and skulked hurriedly down the alley back of the stores and restaurants of C Street. He could hear the dangerous murmurs and pounding feet of those searching for him, and the sounds told him he was in serious trouble.

That trouble would be still more serious if he did not locate Sarah Finley and that agreement. Where could she be?"

Emma Nelson . . . he had seen her with Emma on more than one occasion. She might be at Emma Nelson's cafe. He had to get to the cafe before his pursuers got to him.

The side street was quiet, most pedestrians having gone home for the night. But there was a light in Emma's cafe! Porter grinned mirthlessly to himself.

There'd be two women there, not one, and nothing to prevent him from getting that important paper, the paper that stood between him and serious legal trouble. He hoped Birdie wasn't seriously hurt. That could be a problem for him too, but he always could claim she'd tried to rob him—and, by God, she had!

He paused before the cafe door to catch his breath, then, still breathing hard, he opened the door and entered.

Emma Nelson rose to face him, shielding Sarah behind her, and clutched in Sarah's hand he could see the agreement.

There seemed to be complications. Seated at a table, glaring at him with undisguised hostility, was Belden Ward. And seated opposite Ward, with his black sombrero on his head and his star gleaming, sat the town marshal.

For a long moment there was silence. Then Ward rose and spoke to the heart of the problem. "I don't need your permission to have Sutro proceed, Porter. I've already got permission from your partner—the living one who owns the other half of the Nancy Belle." A glint in his eye, he nodded toward Sarah. "Furthermore, Al, I predict you're going to have a little trouble with Bill Sharon and that loan." He turned. "Marshal, I'm heading out to find Sutro so we can proceed immediately to drain the water from those mines. I'm depending on you to see that this blackguard doesn't do any more damage." He cast a meaningful look at Sarah. "Maybe you'd better give the marshal that agreement—so he can lock it up in the town safe."

As the door slammed behind Ward, Porter still stood there, his face flushed with rage and frustration, glaring at the three before him.

Three? There were four. From the kitchen, where he had

scurried on Porter's entrance, Ed Musgrove, brave in his plaid
suit, gleaming cane, and bowler with its ivory toothpick in its
band; and, standing partly behind Emma Nelson's ample form
for protection, he leaned over and stuck out his tongue at
Porter.

"Ya-a-ah!" said Mr. Musgrove triumphantly.

Porter swore vehemently and lunged forward, only to check
himself before he reached Emma Nelson's immovable form, as
stern and solid a barrier as a granite cliff of the Sierra. Mr.
Musgrove, grinning uncontrollably, scurried back into the
kitchen; and Al Porter, growling, left the restaurant.

Belden Ward located Adolf Sutro in his hotel room and,
although he was fast asleep at the near-midnight hour when
Ward pounded on his door, he was willing and eager to
respond.

"You do not know how happy this makes me!" he exclaimed, shaking Ward's hand vigorously. "It vill take me but
a moment. I vill not shave. I vill go quickly to *mein* tunnel *und*
start *der* vinze. *Und* you say dot *Herr* Porter vill not oppose
und vill not sue?"

"I'm saying that the Finley girl, who's half owner of the
Nancy Belle, has requested you to proceed."

"But—" Sutro drew back, "Porter—"

"Trust me," Ward assured. "I'm on my way now to see Bill
Sharon. And I promise that Al Porter will cause you no
trouble!"

Sutro looked at Ward with understanding. "I vill not ask
how you plan to do this," he said, "but I know you vill succeed." Hustling into his long coat, with collar open he moved
toward the door. There he reached back and shook Ward's
hand once more. "You are a humane man, *Meinherr*."

Ward watched him go, then descended to the hotel lobby
and went back to Sharon's office.

It was now after midnight, and the office was dark. Ward
did not let that deter him, but stomped off down the street

toward the other end of the night-quiet town to the curlicued and furbelowed Victorian house occupied by Bill Sharon and his servants.

The house was dark, and an angry nightshirted butler holding a lighted candle answered the door.

Ward was blunt: "I want to see Bill Sharon."

"He's asleep! He's not to be disturbed!"

"Disturb him," said Ward. "The word I bring is important. Go wake him up."

More argument was required to persuade the butler, but he finally acceded and climbed the stairs to the floor above.

"Mr. Sharon will see you," the butler announced when he came down with a surprised look on his face. "It'll take just a minute for him to put on a robe, and he asks that you wait in the library." Following the man into the dark-paneled room, Ward smiled triumphantly. And in a moment Sharon, pulling a silk robe around him, came in, yawning.

"Belden," he said, "if you weren't such a big depositor, I'd tell you to go to hell. But as it is, what do you want?"

"Al Porter borrowed fifty thousand from you on the basis that he's the sole owner of the Nancy Belle. Right?"

Sharon nodded.

"Well, he's not the sole owner. Finley's niece owns half of it, according to a partnership agreement that Porter signed. I've seen it—don't ask me how!" Squinting, he leaned forward over the desk, the green-shaded lamp casting a light that emphasized his strong, square features. "What are you going to do about that loan?" he queried.

"What do you want me to do about it, Belden? Call it in?"

"No. But I'd like mightily for you to threaten to call it in unless Porter agrees to allow Sutro's winze to drain the Nancy Belle." Relieved to have said what he did, he leaned back. "Will you call Al Porter in first thing tomorrow morning and do that for me?" he asked, his body again taut.

"Glad to," Sharon smiled. "Porter's an s.o.b. anyhow. I won't mind at all seeing him uncomfortable."

Ward rose to go. "I'd also like to know what he bought with that fifty thousand. I'm beginning to think maybe I didn't get all I paid for when I bought the Lone Star."

"Yeah? Well, I'll find out for you while I'm working on the other. Now, Belden, how about letting me get some sleep?"

"Okay—if I've got your promise."

Sharon saw him to the door, yawned, stretched, and headed up the stairs to his room.

CHAPTER 22

IT was morning on the western slope of Sun Mountain. The desert sun was already hot despite the early hour, and the crew emerging from the mouth of the Sutro tunnel was perspiring and weary.

Sutro, Ward, and Sarah Finley sat in the small office, listening intently while the engineer evaluated a report from his foreman.

"Rock's harder'n we thought," the man said, wiping sweat from his brow. "We're drivin' as fast as we can, but it'll still be a few more hours. It ain't easy, drillin' up. An' we may need a blast or two."

"But ve can drain *der* mine ven ve reach der t'ousand-foot drift, *nein*?"

The man nodded. "That's one thing we're sure of. The stope at the drifthead at a thousand feet is full o' water from a shaft from the eight-hundred level. The Nancy Belle crews have reported that. If we can reach that stope, we'll be able to clear the eight-hundred-level drift."

Ward took Sarah Finley's cold hand in his. "There's a lot of air in that eight-hundred-level stope, my dear," he said. "They've all said so. We've got to keep the faith."

The girl was silent, not trusting herself to speak. But, eyes moist, she clutched Ward's hand as if seeking strength from his strong, unwavering confidence.

In the gloom of the eight-hundred level, Don Warren tried to bring his brother back to consciousness and failed. Greg was

177

in a coma and, without a miracle, he never would come out of
it.

Over the past several hours, with only the gleam of the
single wall sconce and the one candle in his hat—which he had
replaced twice—reflecting on the oily, quiet surface of the
black water, Don had been thinking of many things.
Repeatedly his thoughts returned to the dark-haired, prim girl
with the perfect oval face whom he had tried to help. Why
hadn't he realized that he had been drawn to her—and she to
him—when they both were up above in the mining office?
Now, here in the depths, Sarah suddenly became very important to him.

With nothing but time to think, he tried to analyze his
thoughts. Was it only his present incarceration and the
knowledge that he seemed doomed to die in this black cavern
that made him emotional about her? Under normal cir-
cumstances, would he not be regarding her in a more objective
light? Again and again he tried to tell himself that a girl he had
just met could not possibly mean anything to him; that what
he was thinking was wishful fantasy he was indulging in to
restore him mentally to a lifetime above. But repeatedly his
mind turned to her sweet face, her troubled eyes, and the
quiet way she carried herself.

He shrugged and sighed—and the sigh reverberated eerily
and frighteningly in the hollow cave. Dear God, why did he
have to dwell on such thoughts when they could never be
realized?

Suddenly the flickering yellow flame of the wall sconce
grew brighter—and died. Now only the dim glow from his cap
light pierced the unbroken gloom of the flooded stope. And
when it died, there would be no way to rekindle it.

He tried not to think about it. It was only a matter of
time—and a short time at that—until the dim glow from his
cap would vanish into nothingness. Then he and Greg would
spend their last hours on earth in the frightening blackness of
the blind.

* * *

"Use blasting powder if drills haf been slowed!" Sutro shouted at his foreman. "Hurry! Ve must not be delayed!"

When he had issued all the orders he thought would help, he went to Sarah Finley's side. "Everyt'ing iss all right, *Liebchen*," he assured.

Sarah smiled a wan look of appreciation to him—and looked to Belden Ward for reassurance. But she thought his face looked grim. And when Ward took Sutro aside and the two talked in low tones, she was sure she had read Ward right.

Again she felt the utter despair that had engulfed her when the last load of men from the Nancy Belle had reached the surface and Don Warren was not among them.

Don Warren had no way of knowing how long they had been in complete blackness. His cap light had gone out some time ago, and he sat next to his brother, balanced on the rough timbers of the cribbing, swallowing constantly to keep the feeling from choking his throat. Greg had moved only twice, and neither move had indicated a nearness to consciousness.

The drift tunnel consumed his thoughts, particularly the possibility of his swimming underwater to safety. But he kept putting the thought out of his mind.

He swallowed again to still the panic in his heart. The darkness was absolute, heavy, overpowering, thick with hopelessness.

He reached down to adjust his boot. His feet had been dangling in the warm water, and the leather felt soggy. Now, suddenly, there was no water there! He reached down farther, felt around his boot sole. The water was receding!

Stolidly he told himself that he must not read too much into this. It might just be a shift in the flood. But if the water did go down appreciably, he and Greg might be able to make their way back through the tunnel to the elevator shaft.

He reached down again and could not touch the surface of

the water. The water was going down fast—so fast that it could not be merely a change in the currents or a minor change in level caused by a shift in the current.

It was going down—down! Heart thumping, making certain that Greg was balanced on the beam, Don slid off into the water. Previously it had been up to his chin. Now, merciful heaven, it was at the level of his ankles.

It was receding. The flood was being drained. Maybe it was Sutro, maybe some natural cause, but the flood was vanishing. The water gurgled now as it flowed toward the wall of the stope. A secondary benefit: The blackness no longer seemed so threatening. For the first time in hours, he felt a surge of hope.

He reached up and tapped Greg's shoulder. "Greg, boy," he murmured, momentary joy in his voice, "I think we're going to be all right!"

At the headquarters shack of the Nancy Belle, Belden Ward and Sarah Finley confronted Al Porter.

"Sutro's draining your mine," Ward said grimly. "Now you get a crew together and see if you can find those boys at the eight-hundred level."

"What right did that damn Dutchman have to go against my orders? He can whistle for his money, I say! I'll sue the living hell out of him!" Porter yelled.

"You're not going to sue anybody," Ward said quietly. You'll be lucky to stay out of jail! Which reminds me, Bill Sharon wants to see you—today. But before you go, round up your crew."

"You and Bill Sharon can go to hell!" Porter shouted. "And get out of here—both of you!"

Sarah flinched, but Ward did not budge. He stood with legs spread, his blocky body unmoving, his square jaw firm, his cold, blue eyes staring Porter down.

"You're talking to Miss Finley, who's half owner of this mine," said Ward calmly. "And after you see Bill Sharon, you may find out she's the sole owner!"

Porter's mouth was open to roar again—but Ward's last sentence stopped him.

"Whatcha talkin' about?" he demanded.

"Go see Bill Sharon and find out!" Ward suggested. "On second thought," he said, turning to the girl, "we don't need this man's help. You know who to call to round up a crew. Get Flaherty, or somebody."

Sarah cast one more fearful look at Porter, then moved toward the door.

Ward's eyes followed her out. Then he turned and faced Porter again. "If you know what's good for you, you'll get to Bill Sharon," he said. Then he, too, turned on his heel and left the office.

Alone and in a blue rage, Porter swore vitriolically, seized the water carafe on his desk, and smashed it on the floor.

In two hours the word was out that the Nancy Belle was open and looking for a crew, and to speed up the process, the elevator operator fired the boiler and blew the steam from it in a steady, triumphant blast of reveille. Excited miners responded in droves, plodding up the hill and gathering in talkative groups.

Clad in dungarees and wearing a candle cap on his head, Ward marched to the head of the elevator. "Got enough steam to run that thing?" he demanded. And when the elevator man nodded, he called out, "Then let's go!" Alongside Flaherty —the big Irishman who was champing to get under way —the two recruited half a dozen others onto the elevator.

Sarah ran forward. "Can I go? Please!" she begged.

Ward studied her, as if making up his mind. Then the thought prevailed that what they might find might not be to their liking. He shook his head. "We'll bring them up," he told her kindly. "But you wait for us here."

Belden Ward was not the sort one argued with. So, with another blast of the steam whistle, the operator dropped the platform out of sight.

* * *

At the eight-hundred level, which now was drained save for puddles in depressions on the floor, Don Warren tried to revive his brother.

The blackness was total, and oppressive. Not the slightest glimmer of light. One could not see even the shadow of a hand before one's eyes.

"Greg!" Don pleaded. "Greg, boy! Come to! I think we can make a try at getting out of this place!"

But there was no response save Greg's heavy, uneven breathing—which in itself frightened Don. It was almost as if the boy were gasping away his life.

Don tried for several more minutes to revive his brother but failed. Then, making up his mind, he lifted Greg from the precarious perch he had occupied on the rough timber cribbing and laid him gently on a drier spot on the rocky floor of the stope. Out of breath with exertion, he then turned and made his way toward the tunnel entrance that led to the elevator.

It now was up to him to find the drift entrance—but after he had left the cribbing, he knew, with a feeling of panic, that he had lost all sense of direction. He moved forward desperately, encountering a rock wall. Had he missed the drift entrance? Had he turned without realizing it? Frantically he felt along the rock. He must be moving away from the tunnel. His stomach tight with fear, he reversed his direction, found only rock before him, moved what he thought must be several yards, and was about to give up.

Suddenly the wall before him gave way. He had found the drift entrance. Now he knew which way to go—at least for a time. But he must not turn into one of the side corridors. One of them—the one he had stumbled into earlier— was ready to cave in. Flaherty said so. Don knew he must not die, now that hope was rising. For if something happened to him, and those on the surface did not know of the flood's receding, Greg was doomed as well.

Don felt the floor of the drift descend. It was the point which had given him trouble earlier—the low point which had been flooded to the roof and had barred his and Greg's way. Again there was water on the floor, and he was wading. The water rose rapidly—to his hips, almost to his shoulders. The dip in the drift had not drained, and he prayed fervently that it was not so deep that it would block his way again.

His hopes were answered. The water got to his shoulders, and though the roof came frighteningly close to its surface, he still could keep his head above water. Hallelujah! In a moment he felt the floor of the drift rising, and—as he scrambled eagerly upward—he again found himself on a rocky floor with no more than puddles to splash through.

There was a turn in the drift, the point where the side tunnel to the abandoned and dangerous working led. He must not—in this frightening, confusing darkness—permit himself to go down the wrong passage.

There was a side passage and two tunnels. Carefully, inching along, he felt his way. He must choose the right one. Had the abandoned passage come off the right or the left side of the drift when he had blundered into it before? It would be hard to know. He had been coming from the other direction.

He halted, fear again welling up in his throat. He kicked lightly at the surface. The wrong passage had loose rocks on it. There seemed to be a few loose rocks here, but he was not sure.

Suddenly he caught his breath and leaned forward, straining to hear.

It sounded like voices in the distance, coming nearer, the noise of men approaching. And suddenly there flickered the light from a moving candle cap—first one, then two, then several. And the beam from a lantern pierced the blackness of the mine.

As the elevator reached the surface, Sarah and the crowd rushed forward. Don Warren, begrimed and stubbly-bearded, stood aside as Belden Ward and Flaherty carried the limp body of Greg between them. As they laid him on a stretcher, Sarah came up to Don and was about to embrace him—but his grimness held her off.

He nodded toward the stretcher, which was being lifted by two miners toward a wagon. "That's my brother," he said. "I shot him. It was an accident—a terrible accident—but I shot him."

She drew back. "*You* shot him?"

"It was war in the drifts. He came from the other side. I wasn't aiming at him."

An expression of horror came into her eyes. "I wanted so to see you," she said, "but—*you* shot him?" She looked at him long and sadly, then turned away and moved toward the stretcher.

Don Warren watched her go, watched her bend over the man on the stretcher who looked surprisingly like himself, watched her as she mounted the wagon seat to ride to the hospital, and took careful note that she did not look back at him.

Belden Ward looked at Don quizzically. He had been going to slap him on the back and suggest a celebration, but something in Don's manner told him it would not be timely.

Ward cleared his throat awkwardly. "You get cleaned up, son, and get some rest. I'm going over to Bill Sharon's and see what kind of deal I really made when I bought the Lone Star."

Don Warren pulled his eyes away from the departing wagon and turned to Ward. "I haven't thanked you properly, sir—but I will."

Ward patted his shoulder. "Go get some rest," he repeated, and moved off down the hill. He was uncomfortable in the presence of emotion, and at that moment not even the clamor of the happy crowd, the cheerful blasts of the Nancy Belle's whistle, or the presence of the man he had saved eased that discomfort, or gave him a feeling of knowing what to say.

CHAPTER 23

"HE'S with a Mr. Porter," the prim male secretary stiffly told Belden Ward at the Bank of California when Ward had asked to see Sharon.

"Good!" Ward grinned. "I'll join them." He pushed past the secretary and moved toward the inner door.

"Now, wait! You can't do that—"

The secretary was horrified, but Ward opened Sharon's office door and entered, closing it behind him.

The secretary had been right. Sharon—seated behind his big desk, a long cigar in his hand—was confronting Porter. Porter stood spraddle-legged with clenched fists before him.

"You lied to me," Sharon was telling Porter. "You told me you were sole owner of the Nancy Belle. I don't lend money to people who lie. I want it back." Glancing up, he saw Ward. "Oh, hello, Belden," he said. "You've come at the right moment. Come in and sit down."

Ward pulled up a chair.

Sharon did not invite Porter to do the same.

"I found out what Porter bought with that fifty thousand I loaned him," Sharon told Ward. "He said it was for a legitimate survey, which it was. What he really bought was the honest survey which the Lone Star and the Nancy Belle had commissioned to determine the claim line. Cobden had doctored it to give the Lone Star more than its share, and it was the doctored survey that Porter and Finley had been using. When Cobden sold the Lone Star to you, Belden, he

185

thought he'd squeeze out a little more profit from Porter by selling him the real survey, which gave Nancy Belle a claim to a big part of that bonanza. That was what the fifty thousand was for. But"—he turned accusingly to Porter—"this rascal borrowed from me under false pretenses. He told me he owned the entire Nancy Belle. He didn't. I want my money back—now! Or"—he glared at Porter—"I'll put you in jail, Al."

Porter struggled to speak. "I haven't got it!" he said. "I gave it to Cobden. I don't know where the hell Cobden is."

"Neither do I," said Sharon smoothly but with menace in his voice. "But I didn't lend it to Cobden. I lent it to you. And I want it back, or I'll immediately instruct my attorneys to throw the book at you."

Porter swallowed. "I can't do it," he said, his voice rasping with fear. "I'm strapped. That was why I had to borrow in the first place. But I'm good for it, Mr. Sharon!" His voice took on a pleading tone. "I'm good for it! I'll pay you! Give me some time! What I bought means I'll be rich!"

Sharon's voice was cold. "You've got till three o'clock this afternoon, Al. If I don't have the money by that time, I'll act. And don't try to leave town. As soon as you leave my office, I'm going to tell the marshal all about this little deal. So if you can't raise the cash, stay here and take your medicine. If you don't, I'll chase you all over the country if I have to." He sucked his cigar deliberately, blew out a cloud of fragrant blue smoke, and watched it drift toward the paneled ceiling.

"My God," Porter said, "ain't you a human being? You've done things yourself! Give me a chance, will you?"

Sharon glanced at Ward. "Should I give him a chance, Belden?"

"No," said Ward grimly. "This rat doesn't deserve a chance. He was willing to kill two men for the sake of his lousy pocketbook. But"—he winked at Sharon—"I'll give him fifty thousand dollars, and then he can pay you off, Bill."

Porter's jaw dropped, and Sharon smiled. "You—you'll give me fifty thousand?" Porter asked.

"Absolutely. If you'll arrange for a bank draft, Bill, we'll transfer the money from my account into Porter's and wind it up."

"But"—Porter knew the whole story had not been told— "but what do you want for your fifty thousand? What's the catch?"

Ward sat back and grinned. "Your share of the Nancy Belle."

There was a long and tense silence. Again Porter turned purple.

"Fifty thousand!" Porter screamed. "Why, my share's worth millions! It's worth more'n the Yellow Jacket! Fifty thousand! What kind of a fool do you think I am?"

"You're the kind of fool who wants to stay out of prison," Ward said quietly. "Because that's where you'll be if you don't take this offer. More than that, I'll spread the story of how you and Cobden tried to defraud me. I guarantee neither of you'll ever be able to do business again in this country. I've got connections." He stood up. "I haven't got all day. I don't even have the patience of my friend here, and I'm not willing to wait until three o'clock. I want an answer now. You've heard my offer. Take it or leave it. *Now!*"

Porter looked frantically around, like an animal seeking escape from a trap. He turned to Sharon and met an icy stare. Porter swallowed, choking.

"*Now!*" Ward repeated and made as if to turn toward the door.

There was a long silence as Sharon and Ward stared at the trembling, white-faced Porter.

"Better take it," Sharon advised. "Fifty thousand's better than nothing you'll get if I haul you into court. When all this comes out, it's just possible people may conclude you *didn't* shoot your partner in self-defense."

The silence continued. Ward and Sharon glanced at each other, and Ward seemed about to speak, then—

"All right!" Porter said finally, thrusting out the words with effort. "All right! Damn you—both of you! Damn you both to hell! What do I have to do?"

Ward turned to Sharon. "Can you get your secretary to fix up the papers, Bill? As soon as possible."

Sharon said nothing, but rang a bell which brought the young man with the pince-nez and the severe expression into the room. The secretary glared at Ward as he entered, received his instructions, and departed to prepare the papers.

The three sat waiting, silently. Sharon blew a cloud of blue smoke toward the ceiling. "Cigar, Belden?" he asked, extending a box.

"Thanks," said Ward, reaching for one. "Don't mind if I do."

Sharon closed the box and withdrew it.

He did not pass it to Al Porter.

CHAPTER 24

A month passed. The sign over the Lone Star, which had previously bore the inscription, JAS. COBDEN, PROP., now had the words, BELDEN WARD, PROP. And the sign over the administration shack of the Nancy Belle now read FINLEY AND WARD, PROPS.

But Don Warren no longer sat at his desk in the outer office of the Nancy Belle. He now occupied Cobden's office at the Lone Star Mine, and with it the title of manager of all of Belden Ward's Nevada properties. Sarah Finley also had made a move—into the inner office of the Nancy Belle.

Other things had changed as well. Greg Warren now was ambulatory and was regaining his normal weight. Almost every day Sarah Finely seemed to bring him flowers and tidbits from Emma Nelson's kitchen, and frequently, after office hours, they were seen taking walks together down C Street.

One morning, at nine o'clock, Greg came into his brother's new office at the Lone Star.

"You look great," Don greeted him cheerfully, "As if you're about ready to go back to work! And speaking of work, I've been talking to Mr. Ward, and because he's expanding his interests in Washoe—and put me in charge of 'em all—I'll need an assistant. Ward's agreed. And we've got a salary offer for you."

He began rummaging in his desk for Ward's latest letter.

Greg interrupted him. "Don," he said seriously, "this is just like all the other conversations we've had lately. We never seem to talk about anything important. It's as if we're afraid of something."

"What's more important than a job?" Don asked, forcing a laugh.

"I'll tell you what's more important: Sarah."

Don looked uncomfortable. "I don't want to talk about her," he said.

"But today we're going to."

"Why should I?" Don asked, tightening his jaw. "When she found out I was responsible for your problems, she turned against me—just like that!" He snapped his fingers.

"She's a girl, Don—and she was shocked. She's had a bad time of it here, with her uncle murdered, Porter trying to do her out of her legacy, the flood in the mine—"

Don's eyes showed their hurt, but his words were stubborn. "Sarah's become one of the richest women in the Comstock, and I'm not interested in rich women. If I ever get married, *I* want to be the boss in my family. Anyway, Greg"— he lifted his gaze directly into his brother's eyes—"she's no longer interested in me. She wants *you*. She's been with you every day since we came out of that hole. And I've forgotten her. I'll admit it was hard to do, but I have. Let's change the subject."

"No, Don, I've got a little more to say. I'm not taking the job as your assistant. I'm going back to San Francisco. Ward can find me something else to do, because I'm leaving."

Don stared at him in astonishment. "Why, for God's sake? A good job here, the prettiest and richest girl in Washoe yours for the asking—You're crazy!"

Greg slowly shook his head. "She's not mine for the asking, Don." He stood up. "Look at me, look at my face. We're an awful lot alike."

Don hesitated. "What are you saying?"

"Every time Sarah looks at me, she sees you. Every time she talks to me, she's talking to you. Words slip out. She calls me 'Don' half the time. She asks about you. She presses me all the time on what really happened down there. I've told her it was dark and confused and that you certainly didn't intend to shoot anybody. I've told her our positions could have been completely reversed in that howling fracas and that nobody should hold anything against you and that I certainly don't. I've argued with her on that point dozens of times. Now I think she's beginning to believe it. I catch her looking out the window at your office door. She's even called on me a couple of times before five o'clock so she could watch you come out and walk down the hill." He paced the floor as he talked. "I like Sarah," he continued, "but I'm not for her. I'm going back to San Francisco."

There was a long silence as Don sat drumming his fingers on the desk. Finally he spoke up. "You're just saying that, aren't you?" he said. "You're making it all up. You really want her, but you think I do too. So you're pulling out—"

Greg shook his head and smiled. "Your words couldn't be farther from the truth. I don't want to marry a woman and have her call me 'Don' all my life—every time she forgets herself. Sarah's nice, but—hell, she's older than I am! Two years! Believe me, I've never been more honest in my life!"

Don, too, had risen, and now he rounded his desk and gripped his brother's arm. "I've hurt you enough," he said. "I don't want to hurt you again. I know you like Sarah—"

Greg smiled sadly. "I don't know what it takes to convince you, Don. Believe me, I mean what I say. Every word!" He moved toward the door. "I thought you might be tough to convince, so I'm taking action. I'm on the afternoon stage. I've already told Sarah, and I can tell you—she's not broken up."

Wordlessly, Don shook his brother's hand, then watched as Greg strode down the hill, his booted heels raising little puffs of yellow dust. And though Don watched him all the way to the foot of the hill, not once did Greg look back.

That same day, a little before noon, Don Warren and Sarah Finley entered Emma Nelson's cafe and seated themselves at the counter. Emma, emerging from her kitchen, stared at them. "Well!" she exclaimed, obviously at a loss for words.

Don grinned at her—the first time he had smiled so broadly

in days. "I'll bet the question you were going to ask is, 'Have you two buried the hatchet?' Well, I can tell you: The answer is 'Yes.' " He looked at Sarah, and she smiled back. "Now we're here to celebrate. Tell me: What have you got on the menu that's fitting?"

"Well," said Emma doubtfully, frowning in thought so that her ample face developed even more folds and bulges than usual, "I got pot roast an' gravy. But"—her face brightened—"I also just baked a mince pie—an' it's good! I'll fix some brandy sauce for ye an' light it as I serve it!"

Sarah laughed—a happy, lilting sound—and reached for Don's hand beneath the counter's edge. "That'll be fine, Emma," she said. "I know your pot roast—and it'll be just as good as the mince pie."

The door slammed, and two other customers entered. The three turned to see who they were. It was Mr. Musgrove, again in his plaid suit, jauntily swinging his shiny cane. On his arm was Miss Birdie Boynton, clad in purple plush, with a large purple hat adorned with ostrich feathers atop her blond coiffure.

Mr. Musgrove lifted his cane. "Emma," he said, "we're celebratin'! Birdie's finally agreed to go out with me—an' nothin's too good for her!"

"Well," cooed Birdie coyly, adjusting her back hair, "any feller who buys a girl a hat like this deserves a little extree attention, don't you think?"

"I certainly do!" said Sarah. "The hat is beautiful!"

Emma moved her large bulk toward the kitchen door. "Lucky I baked two mince pies," she said. "Now, if I only don't run outa brandy . . . "